THE CHRISTMAS BRIDE

A Burnett Bride Novella

BY SYLVIA MCDANIEL

Books by Sylvia McDaniel

Contemporary Romance

Standalones
The Reluctant Santa
My Sister's Boyfriend
The Wanted Bride
The Relationship Coach
Her Christmas Lie
Secrets, Lies, and Online Dating
Paying for the Past
Cupid's Revenge

Anthologies
Kisses, Laughter & Love
Christmas with you

Collaborative Series

Magic, New Mexico
Touch of Decadence

Western Historicals

Standalones
A Hero's Heart
A Scarlet Bride
Second Chance Cowboy

The Cuvier Women
Wronged
Betrayed
Beguiled

Lipstick and Lead
Desperate
Deadly
Dangerous
Daring
Determined
Deceived

Scandalous Suffragettes
Abigail
Bella
Callie
Faith

The Burnett Brides
The Rancher Takes a Bride
The Outlaw Takes a Bride
The Marshal Takes a Bride
The Christmas Bride

Anthologies
Wild Western Women
Courting the West
Wild Western Women Ride Again

Collaborative Series

The Surprise Brides
Ethan

American Mail Order Brides
Katie

The Christmas Bride
Published by Virtual Bookseller

Cover Design by Kathleen Baldwin

Edited by Andrea Dickinson
http://www.qualitybookservices.com/

Formatted by Laurelle Procter
laurelleprocter@gmail.com

Short Description: Matchmaker Eugenia Burnett is unable to find a woman for Wyatt Jones, because it's Eugenia that he wants.

ISBN: 978-1-942608-52-3 (paperback)
ISBN: 978-1-942608-53-0 (e-book)

{Historical Western Romance – Fiction}

www.SylviaMcDaniel.com

Synopsis

Eugenia Burnett has gotten what she wants. Her three sons are married and she has three grandchildren, with the fourth on the way. But she hasn't given up her matchmaking ways. Now she's moved on to the people she knows and she's matching widows and widowers together. Until one widower, Wyatt Jones let's her know in front of a crowded restaurant that he's not interested in any of the women she keeps sending him except her. Sworn never to remarry, she doesn't need a husband or want one. She's a free spirit doing what she pleases and no one is going to boss her around. But Wyatt wants Eugenia and she says no.

In this western historical romance novella, come back to the old west and spend Christmas with the Burnett family. See Eugenia meet her match in cowboy Wyatt Jones.

Table of Contents

Chapter One

"June told me you're good at helping a woman find a husband," Myrtle Sanders said, her voice soft and barely discernible over the clank of dishes and customers' voices in the café in Fort Worth, Texas.

Eugenia Burnett's ears hurt from the last hour of Myrtle's continuous whining about how her children didn't visit her and how loneliness was her only companion.

Her story had begun to grate on Eugenia's nerves like ants scurrying along a trail until she was ready to tell the woman she had to run. Literally, she wanted to escape.

Finally, like an overdue stagecoach, the conversation seemed to have arrived at the reason Myrtle had asked her to lunch.

"Much to my children's dismay, I do enjoy dabbling in helping people find a partner," Eugenia admitted, her mind already thinking of the possible matches for Myrtle. She'd find her a man.

Eugenia smiled, her heart warming at the thought of her sons and their families. Since she'd found mates for her three stubborn boys, she'd begun to help her friends find mates to spend the rest of their days with.

The woman smiled, her eyes full of doubt. "What's the chance of either one of us ever marrying again?"

"Me?" Eugenia asked, stunned. What had she said that gave this woman the impression she wanted a husband? She needed to disavow this notion immediately.

"I'm not looking to get hitched to any man. I don't need the aggravation of being married. I'm in a mighty nice place. My kids are close. The ranch is run by Travis and Tanner, and I have spending money if I need it. There is nothing that a man can provide that I need."

When Thomas died, the ranch was earning enough she could continue her style of life without her husband. Without a man telling her when to take her next breath.

"Not even companionship?" the woman asked, a pensive pinch to her face.

Eugenia shrugged, remembering those first few desolate nights. "If I get lonely, my grandchildren are close-by. The rest of the time is mine to do what I please."

Myrtle shook her head. "My Charlie use to wrap his arms around me at night and hold me close. I miss that tenderness."

"He also liked to tell you what you could and couldn't do," Eugenia said, remembering how Thomas ordered her around. She was no longer that pliant bride of fifteen.

"Yes, men seem to think they have to be in control of a woman," Myrtle admitted.

"And I don't need any man to tell me what I can and can't do. I'm quite capable of taking care of myself."

Long gone were the days when Eugenia Burnett took orders from any man. Now she was a strong woman capable of voicing her opinion and making her own decisions.

Myrtle sighed. "Sometimes Charlie was a little overbearing, but there were times I could change his mind. At this age, a good man is hard to find. I'm lonely. I don't like living by myself. I want a man to take care of me."

"Don't worry. I'm certain I can help you. Just last month I helped Claudine meet Richard. I also introduced Mary to Loyd and then there was June and Dillon. Women our age can find a man if we want one," Eugenia assured Myrtle.

Though the sparkle of youth had faded, Eugenia's friends claimed they were lonely and needed mates at their sides. Matching up widow women entertained her and kept her busy, much to her sons' dislike.

Myrtle leaned in closer. "You certainly like to match people up. I mean look at your sons. You put them together with their wives."

"Someone had to, or I would never have had any grandkids. They didn't seem inclined to find women to settle down with, so I took action to get what I wanted. Grandkids. Now I have two boys and a girl with another one on the way."

"You are a determined woman."

Eugenia almost laughed out loud. Now she was a determined woman, but in her youth…she'd been a milquetoast bride. Not any longer.

"I go after what I want, and most of the time I get my way." Eugenia lifted her chin defiantly. Since Thomas passed away, she'd relished in her freedom. She'd grown strong and hard as nails and wielded her matriarchal power over her sons.

"Myrtle, what do you want? Do you want another man telling you what to do?" Eugenia asked.

"I want someone by my side. I want to roll over in the middle of the night and reach out to feel a man beside me. I want to smile across the dinner table and have someone to talk to."

The noise from the café seemed to fade into the background as Eugenia stared at Myrtle's brown hair streaked with strands of gray and her milky complexion lined with wrinkles.

"Let me think about who is available," Eugenia said as she thought of the eligible widowers and single men in town that she knew. "Red Jenkins's wife just died, so it's too soon for him. James Randall has been a widower for six months, but he has a fondness for drink. Bart Smith has been a widower for a year, but his children still live with him. You would be taking on the care of two older kids.

Then there is Wyatt Jones. He was married to my friend Beatrice."

Eugenia's heart quivered at the thought of big Wyatt.

"I know Wyatt. He's one big cowboy. One that certainly makes a woman's pulse race," Myrtle said, her blue eyes wide and dreamy with the possibility.

Eugenia nodded her head. Yes, she thought so, too. "He's quite the catch. A mite stubborn, but he took great care of Beatrice when she was ill. Wyatt's all bullheaded man."

Myrtle whispered softly. "What would you recommend I do?"

"Simple. Make him a casserole dish and take it out to his place. After all, it's just him and the ranch hands. As far as I know, he doesn't have anyone making him home-cooked meals. Men love a good meal."

Men were so gullible. A home-cooked meal and the romance was on.

Myrtle grinned, her blue eyes shining with tears. "Charlie always loved my chicken and rice. Do I just drop it off?"

"Sure. It's a signal that you're interested in him. You take him the casserole, you smile, and tell him you hope to see him in town soon. That's a subtle way of saying you'd like him to ask you out to dinner. If he doesn't respond, then you try again."

Myrtle stared at her, a frown creased her forehead. "What if he just looks at me? What do I do then?"

"Oh, he's smart enough to know what you're implying. If he doesn't respond by the second casserole, then we'll have to find someone else."

And Wyatt had turned down more than one woman with a casserole she'd sent his way. Sooner or later, he would take the bait.

Myrtle frowned, her eyes wrinkling in the corners. "You're sure about this?"

"It's how Mary and Loyd met."

The door to the café opened, the cold wind slamming it against the wall. The restaurant grew quiet with the sudden entrance, and Eugenia turned to see who was making such a racket.

Wyatt Jones stood in the doorway, his muscular frame filling the opening. His cowboy hat sat at an angle on top of his head, and his large brown eyes scanned the room.

In his hand, he carried a duffle bag.

Eugenia tried to ignore the big man as he strolled through the doorway and removed his Stetson.

Their gazes locked across the room, and he smiled, his full lips turning up in a grin that made her body soften and her heart give an extra little ca-thunk. He spoke to the waitress, but his gaze never wavered from Eugenia.

Uh-oh. A tingle of nerves zinged through her bones. This couldn't be good.

His boots made a rhythmic thump, thump, thump on the wooden floor as he walked with a determined stride straight toward her, his bag in hand, his spurs jingling. Nervously, she licked her lips.

Myrtle's back faced the door, and she continued to blather about something. But Eugenia couldn't seem to focus on the words. All she could see was this handsome cowboy walking her way. She couldn't stop staring at him. She knew he was coming for her.

She'd already sent several women his way, and she didn't think he was here to thank her for curing his loneliness.

Wyatt stopped at their table, touching the rim of his hat as he glanced at Myrtle. "Morning Mrs. Sanders. Nice to see you."

He pivoted to Eugenia, his brown eyes dancing with merriment. Staring into those earthy eyes, a warm flush settled over her like a blanket. He opened the bag, withdrew a casserole dish, and laid it on the table. He took a second dish out and placed it alongside the first one, and then another, and another.

Oh dear.

When he finished, six clean, empty casserole dishes sat in front of her.

His mouth turned up in that slow, lazy grin that burned a sizzle along her spine. Why did this man make her feel like she'd raced her grandchildren around the yard and couldn't catch her breath? Why did this man make her more nervous than a virgin on her wedding day? Why did this man have her wondering how his lips would feel against her own?

"Eugenia," he said in that deep drawl that sent shivers skittering over her. "You've been mighty busy, sending women out to my house. You've kept me and my men well fed the last couple of weeks."

"Glad I could help," she said, her voice sounding breathy and soft.

He leaned in close and put his hands on either side of her, effectively pinning her in the chair. She felt the urge to jump up and run, but resisted. She sat there, stared him in the eye and refused to back down. No longer would she back down to any man. Never again.

"While I appreciate the effort, I'm not taking the bait. There's only one woman in this town that I'm interested in pursuing to become my wife." The deep timbre of his voice was low and commanding.

"And pray tell, who would that be?" she asked, knowing she would have him hitched as soon as possible.

"You, Eugenia Burnett. You."

His cinnamon eyes twinkled with amusement and left her tingly in places she refused to acknowledge.

The heat from the fireplace warmed the room, but she sat frozen in her chair, unable to move, unable to respond. Wyatt Jones wanted her to become his wife?

"Think about it."

Before her mouth began to work again, he rose, picked up his bag, turned, and walked out of the restaurant.

Slowly her body seemed to come to life again and with it her resolve. He'd be waiting until hell froze over if he thought she would marry him.

~

Inside the Burnett homestead kitchen, Rose Burnett glanced around the table at her sisters-in-law. Eugenia was outside playing with Lucas and Desirée while the women had a rare moment alone.

"Hey, did y'all hear what happened at the cafe?"

Sarah started to laugh. "Did I hear? Tucker came in laughing about how his mother may have finally met her match."

Beth looked confused. "What happened?" Rose and Sarah told her how Wyatt Jones had confronted Eugenia at the café.

"He said he wanted to marry her?" Rose asked, her voice low.

"Said she was the only woman he was interested in pursuing is what I heard," Sarah replied.

Beth about snorted her coffee. "Wow! I don't know how Tanner would feel about his mother remarrying. How about Tucker and Travis?"

Rose smiled. "Oh, Travis thinks his mother needs someone to keep her under control. Since she lied to bring us together and said I stole her wedding ring, he's thinking maybe she needs someone to make certain she minds her own business."

Though Rose was grateful to Eugenia for bringing them together, during that time, Travis had made her life miserable.

Sarah rolled her eyes. "The way she lied to me about my grandfather being ill. It's very hard to believe everything she says. I know she brought me home with the hope that Tucker and I would work out our differences." She rubbed her hand across her swollen stomach. "I'm glad that she did, but when I got off that stage and learned that grandfather wasn't seriously ill, I would have gladly strangled that woman."

"I never would have met Tanner if it wasn't for her," Beth acknowledged quietly. "Though I almost wound up with Tucker, now I'm grateful to her."

"Yes, but don't you think she deserves the same happiness that we have with our husbands?" Rose asked, thinking that her mother-in-law deserved her own chance at happiness. "Thomas Burnett has been dead for well over five years. It would be better for her to have a man she could focus her attention on rather than her sons."

"And grandchildren," Beth said.

"And matchmaking. You did hear that she has sent six women to Wyatt's place with casserole dishes," Sarah volunteered.

Rose giggled like a young girl, thinking of Eugenia's reaction to Wyatt's casserole dish display. The gossip had spread faster than cholera through town. "I would love to have witnessed her reaction when Wyatt laid out all those empty casserole dishes in front of her."

"Has she mentioned Wyatt? Do you think she's interested in getting married again?" Beth asked.

Sarah shook her head. "Oh no, she wants nothing to do with getting married herself. She told Tucker at dinner the other night that there was no way that she would saddle herself with another husband. One was enough."

There was a group sigh, and for a moment everyone sat there in silence. Finally, Beth said, "Did either of you want to get married?"

The other two women shook their heads.

"No way," Rose responded, remembering her dreams of being like her mother, an actress on the stage.

"Not really," Sara replied. "I had my son and my practice, what more could I need?"

"Yet, when we fell in love, we wanted to marry our husbands," Rose said.

"And how did we meet our husbands?" Beth asked.

"Eugenia," the three women responded in unison. They laughed.

"How do we help her fall in love?" Rose asked, trying to remember when she realized she loved Travis. They had fought each other and the feeling for so long that when they finally succumbed, it was euphoric.

Sara grinned. "We do what Mama Burnett did. Every chance we get, we wrangle them together."

Rose leaned back and laughed. Eugenia wouldn't let Travis arrest her again, so she'd stayed at the ranch because of Eugenia. "Wyatt hasn't been to the ranch recently. We'll invite him for dinner next weekend. Beth and I will plan everything, and you and Tucker can come out. The whole family will get to meet Mr. Jones."

"You know, there's the annual Christmas tree event coming up soon. Let's do everything we can to arrange for them to be in the same wagon," Beth said, laughing gleefully.

"The meeting about the Christmas pageant is in two weeks. Eugenia said she was going to volunteer again to be the pageant director," Sarah said, unable to contain a giggle.

"But this year, Mr. Davis passed away. They need a new coordinator. Wonder if we can convince Wyatt he would make an excellent organizer," Rose said excitedly.

They laughed.

Sara nodded at her sisters-in-law. "Sometimes what we do can come back to haunt us. This time Eugenia is going to meet her match."

Rose nodded, thinking poor Eugenia was going to get quite a surprise. "This time we're doing the matchmaking."

~

Wyatt looked over at Gus, his ranch foreman, the man who'd been at his side for nearly twenty years. Since Beatrice's death, Wyatt had taken to eating in the bunkhouse with the men rather than up at the large, empty house he rumbled around in.

After dinner, he and Gus usually came back to the house where they would share a whiskey or two before they each headed off to bed.

"It's December, and already that north wind is colder than a well-digger's ass in Montana," Gus said, backing up to the blaze, warming his backside.

Tonight was cold, and Wyatt had started a fire in the hearth to chase the chill from the study. He'd refused to let Beatrice decorate this one room. This room belonged to him, and he'd decorated it just the way he damn well pleased. Now, he wanted to move his bed in here rather than sleep in that lonely bedroom upstairs. He missed his wife, the healthy Beatrice, not the woman who'd wasted away before his eyes.

"Yes, we probably need to have the men go ahead and move the cattle to the south pasture, where we can keep an eye on them. Looks like winter arrived early this year."

Books graced the shelves along with liquor bottles. Above the fireplace mantel hung his ten-point buck he'd shot right after they built the house. This house, his home, held so many memories, and now he was ready to create more memories with someone, maybe even Eugenia.

"Yap," Gus responded and then rubbed his belly. "I was getting spoilt to those casseroles you kept bringing out. What happened? They've dried up worse than the creek in summer."

"I put an end to them," Wyatt responded, remembering the look on Eugenia's face as he'd pulled out the empty dishes. Sometimes a man had to get the upper hand, and he'd taken the first step that day.

"Dang, I was enjoying a woman's cooking for a change."

"Then I'll give you the women's names and you can call on them," Wyatt admonished, taking a swig of his drink.

Gus rolled his eyes. "And end up hog tied to one of 'em? No, thanks. You're used to a woman, and since Miss Beatrice has been gone a year, maybe you should consider one of these fine ladies who are cooking you casseroles."

Wyatt set his glass down and considered his friend. Funny how a man who'd never married could give him advice on finding a woman. "The problem is that none of them interest me."

"Dang, that's a real shame. I was enjoying their cooking. Could you at least string them along for a little while, so we can continue to eat decent food?" Wyatt slammed his drink on the desk. "Now, what kind of man does that to a woman?"

Gus was a great foreman, a good man who didn't know how to handle women. Never had been able to keep a woman interested in him longer than a courting moon. Maybe there was a reason he'd never married. A hungry man?"

"Go to the damn café if you're hungry. Don't depend on widow women who are looking husbands, unless you want to get hitched," Wyatt told him.

"No, thanks!" Gus held up his hand and shook his head. "You have to admit we haven't had food like that since Mrs. Beatrice died."

Beatrice had been an excellent cook. They'd eaten well, and her pies were known for bringing the men running in from the barn. But she was gone. "Well, it's over. I put a stop to the widow women's cooking."

Gus sank into a chair across from him and laughed. "Why did all these women think you were on the hunt for a wife?"

"From what I was told, they were sent here by Eugenia Burnett." He couldn't help but think about Eugenia. Her dark hair was more silver than black, and her blue eyes sparkled with heat and laughter. For being almost fifty, her figure was still neat and trim in a shorter spitfire version.

"Mrs. Beatrice's friend?"

"The one." The woman was a small ball of dynamite that no one wanted to cross.

Gus stammered in shock. "W-we-ell why would she be trying to set up her friend's husband?" Wyatt shrugged and contemplated the fire. "You know we often had Eugenia and Thomas out for dinner."

Eugenia and he shared something that they had never acknowledged while they were both married. At a dinner, they'd accidentally touched, and Wyatt's body had tingled and hummed with something he'd never experienced before. While he was married to Beatrice, he'd avoided his wife's best friend.

"Yes, those two women could talk the feathers off a chicken."

Wyatt took a sip of his whiskey, letting it warm him all the way to his toes, just like a fine woman could heat up a man. And that's what he missed. He missed having a woman. Her soft touches, tender smiles, and gentle reminders. It was the little things that he took for granted.

He missed having a strong-willed woman who would stand up to him and challenge him to become a better man.

After spending the day around men, he missed coming home to a woman's voice, her smell, the way she eased his burdens.

"You haven't answered my question. Why is Eugenia trying to find you a wife?"

"Maybe because when our mates were alive, there was always this mindfulness between us. Nothing ever happened of course, but we felt drawn to one another."

Nothing ever happened, but now that Beatrice had been gone a year, he wanted to set fire to that ember in Eugenia. There was something there that he wanted to create a blazing inferno with. Even thinking about her made his gut tighten and blood rush to his groin.

Gus's brows rose as he looked at Wyatt over his drink. "Are you crazy? That woman is known for her meddling. They call her the meddling matchmaker. Why in the hell Eugenia? Why not some sensible woman?"

Wyatt leaned toward Gus. "Oh, Eugenia's sensible all right. She's strong willed and wouldn't cower every time I raised my voice to her like most women. Give me a woman who knows what she wants and goes after her desires rather than one who lays around with the damn vapors all day."

"Beatrice—"

"Beatrice was great until she got sick. Then all I could do was sit by and watch her waste away. Both of us died a little bit every day. Her body and my heart. But she's gone."

Three years of being ill and then she'd gone like a thief in the night, quiet and quick, leaving behind her grief-stricken family. Now over twelve months had passed, and he was ready to move on.

"God rest her soul." Gus raised his glass in the air to Beatrice and then put it to his lips and gulped. "Still, you and Eugenia Burnett. I'm so damn shocked I can't feel my face anymore."

"You can't feel your face because of the whiskey."

"That too. But Eugenia? Slap me upside the head. You've got your spurs tangled up. Is she interested in you?"

Wyatt shrugged. "Who knows? I told her she was the only woman I wanted to get a casserole from."

"She hasn't brought one yet," Gus said.

Oh, Eugenia Burnett would not be that easy. No, courting Eugenia would be tricky and so much fun.

"She's not going to, either. It's going to take a little more persuasion on my part before she'll come around. Eugenia's not some young filly ready to be bred. Nope, she's going to require some top-notch wooing."

Gus laughed. "The idea of you chasing a woman at your age is pretty funny."

"That better be the whiskey talking. I'm still young enough to want a woman in my bed. I'm still young enough that I don't want some wimpy woman who is just going to lie there and endure. Eugenia will make a great wife. She'll make life interesting again."

"Lord, boss, if she's what you want, I hope you're right. If not, you're going to spend the rest of your days living in marriage hell."

"Or it could be damn near heaven."

Chapter Two

Eugenia watched as her children and grandchildren scurried about the living area of the ranch house. Her grandchildren playing tag around the Sheraton sofa and the rocking chair. The main room was filled with her sons and their families for the second week in a row. Normally everyone was so busy that they decided the first Sunday of the month was family day, and they all gathered on that day. But it was Saturday. There were no birthdays, and the holidays were still weeks away. Her motherly instincts were on full alert, and her female intuition kept screaming something's up. Her children were being very tight-lipped.

"Rose," Eugenia called. "Can I speak to you?"

"Sorry, Eugenia. It's going to have to wait," she said and hurried into the kitchen to help Cook with the meal. She flittered about as nervous as a June bug searching for light on a moonless night.

Rose could evade her questions, but Beth had just walked into the parlor and she couldn't lie.

Eugenia walked up to Beth. "Why is everyone here? What's going on?"

Beth's emotions were so easy to read. She licked her lips and glanced back at her husband as if seeking his support. "Nothing. We're just waiting for our guest to arrive."

"Guest? No one said anything about a guest. I wondered why everyone had gathered for dinner. Who's coming over?" Eugenia asked, stunned they hadn't said a word about the visitor.

Beth's face blanched and her eyes widened. "I'm sorry, Eugenia. I think I hear the baby crying. I need to go check on Seth."

Eugenia watched as Beth scurried away faster than a mouse with a cat on its tail. Her children were definitely hiding something.

She walked over to Travis, determined to learn who her children had invited to dinner. "This is quite unusual for all of us to get together for dinner two weeks in a row."

Travis smiled. "We all thought it would be good to get together."

So they were trying to keep the guest's identity a secret. She narrowed her gaze at her oldest son and raised her brows at him as if he were five. "I'm your mother. Who is coming to dinner?"

Travis grinned that same smile he'd used as a boy when he thought he'd pulled a fast one. "The girls invited Wyatt Jones to dinner tonight."

Her heart leaped and began an erratic beat in her throat.

"What?" She put her hands on her hips. "For God's sake, why?"

"Because the girls invited Wyatt," Travis said as if she was a simpleton who didn't understand. A knock sounded on the door. "In fact, I think that's him now."

With startling clarity, she suddenly realized her family had heard about the incident at the café, and now they were trying to help Wyatt in his quest to lure her into marriage. Lure her into another man controlling her every move.

There wasn't enough gold in California for her to take the bait.

Travis threw open the door. "Wyatt, glad you could make it. Come on in."

Wyatt strode through into the parlor, his large body seeming to fill up the space of the living area. Their gazes met across the room, and he removed his hat. His dark hair was sprinkled with silver in a nice way that complemented his high cheekbones and full lips. For a man in his forties, he still had a trim, strong frame that was both tempting and well defined.

Gosh darn it, why did her body have a second awakening when he came into the room? Why did her heart pound a little faster and her blood rush like a freight train through her veins? She refused to acknowledge that a glance from Wyatt's earthy brown eyes had her body humming with an awareness that she'd long forgotten.

"Evening, Eugenia."

That cognizance of him as a man had happened many years ago, when they were both married. Happily married. He'd accidentally touched her hand at a party, and they'd both jumped from the tingle that had zipped up her hand to her heart. An innocent touch that had them staring at each other with shock. Since that day, she'd avoided him at all costs. Now that he was widowed, she needed to find another widow woman to send his way quick.

"Wyatt," she acknowledged, the memory of their last conversation making her wary. He had that same duffle bag in his hands. He wasn't going to start bringing empty casserole dishes to her home was he? "How are you?"

"Excellent, thanks. I brought some candy I thought you might enjoy." He pulled a sack of penny candy from the bag, and she breathed a sigh of relief. No empty casserole dishes.

"Since Rose is in charge of this party, I'll give them to her," she said, wanting nothing to do with his gift.

"No," he said, his voice gruff. "I brought each of the women a sack of candy. I just wanted to make sure you got yours first," he said, his full lips turning up in a smile that warmed her from the inside out.

A thrill of excitement waltzed down her spine, landing in her center with a box step.

"Oh, thanks," she said, taken back. She loved penny candy. She licked her lips. How could she refuse the little bag? It would be impolite. She'd accept them just this once. "Thanks, Wyatt."

Wyatt smiled at her response, and she knew she had to let him know real quick that this meant nothing. She'd accept his cinnamon candy, just not his proposal.

He was making it very clear to her sons his intentions to court her. She needed to snip this little matchmaking exercise in the bud. Not now. Not ever.

Rose came into the room and smiled at Wyatt. She leaned in to kiss him on the cheek. "So good to see you, Mr. Jones. We're glad you came tonight."

"Thanks for inviting me," he said. "I brought you, Sarah, and Beth a bag of penny candy as well."

"How sweet," she said, glancing at Eugenia. "Thank you."

Eugenia was feeling nauseated as she watched him win over each one of her daughters-in-law. They were so easily bribed by a sweet-talking man. They'd married her sons after all.

"I think dinner is just about ready," Rose said. "We should all make our way to the dining room."

Eugenia tried to hang back and let the other couples go in first, but Wyatt came to her side. "Could I seat you at the dinner table, Eugenia?" he asked, his cinnamon eyes twinkling with amusement.

The man knew exactly what he was doing, and he knew she was not happy about his obvious pursuit in front of her family. She raised her brows at him. "I'm perfectly capable of seating myself, Mr. Jones, but I'll allow you to walk me to the table."

He took her arm and placed her hand in the crook of his elbow and then smiled down at her as if she was on the menu. "Eugenia, I have no doubts about your capabilities. I've been on the receiving end of your endeavors. You're quite good."

"Thank you. I strive to do my best at whatever I do."

"That's good to know."

She narrowed her eyes at him, staring, her heart racing. Why did this man always have the ability to make her body react?

"Let me pull your chair out for you," he said, trying to keep from grinning at her and failing.

The man was insufferable. He was deliberately trying to goad her. Deliberately trying to get a reaction from her. But she refused to take his bait. He would have to work harder if he expected a rise from her.

"Thank you, Wyatt," she said, playing his game. "Tell me, have you received anymore casserole dishes recently?"

"No, I'm quite disappointed. I was hoping to receive your casserole dish."

She laughed as she sank onto the chair he'd pulled out. "My kitchen is closed. I'm not baking for any man."

He leaned in close to her ear. "You don't have to cook for me. But I'd buy a new kitchen for you, if you'd let me."

She sent him her haughtiest stare. "I don't want a new kitchen. I like my life."

Rose cleared her throat. Eugenia glanced up and realized her family was all sitting at the table and they were watching the two of them, their lips pursed to keep from snickering.

She gave her sons her meanest reproving mother look. "Well. Aren't one of you boys going to say the blessing so we can eat?"

～

Wyatt stared across the parlor at the woman he couldn't stop thinking about. They'd been dancing around each other for years, and it was time to either take action or cut bait. Sure, Eugenia wasn't a young woman, but he didn't want a young woman who wanted babies. At this time in his life, he wanted an equal partner. A woman who knew the rough roads of life and would face them with him.

He wanted a woman who would stay with him until he took his last breath. Eugenia was that type of woman.

Her sons seemed accepting of him, and now he wanted to test the boundaries. "Eugenia, would you take a stroll out in the night air with me?"

She raised one brow and stared at him in a sassy manner that clearly said you're crazy.

"It's chilly outside."

She wasn't going to make this easy, and that urged him on. He liked the challenge and hoped the final reward would be as good.

Rose stepped forward. "Here's your shawl. It's a very pretty night out tonight."

Eugenia cut her a look that should have stopped the young woman cold, but Rose ignored the glare sent her direction and handed her mother-in-law the shawl.

"Okay, but let's make it quick." Just long enough to tell Wyatt to stop this madness.

He stood and offered Eugenia his arm. "We'll only be gone as long as you want."

Eugenia rose from the settee and placed her hand in the crook of his arm and then looked at her kids. "This won't take but a moment."

No one said a word as they walked out the door, but as soon he shut the wooden opening, Wyatt heard laughter.

Yes, her family was definitely enjoying watching their courtship.

They walked down the steps and several feet out into the yard, just far enough for privacy. "It's a little nippy for December. I think we're going to have a cold winter this year."

She stopped. Pulled her hand from his arm and pointed her finger at him. "Wyatt Jones, I know what you're up to, and it's not going to happen."

He smiled at her but didn't say a word, standing there in his down coat, felt hat, and leather boots, watching her like she was the evening's entertainment.

"Somehow you've talked Rose into helping you, but I will straighten that out right away. I'm not interested in ever getting married again."

Wyatt shrugged and slipped his hands into his pockets. "And here I thought we were just going to have a nice friendly stroll."

Her defenses were locked in place, and somehow he needed to get through the walls she'd built and show her they could be good together.

"You're trying to court me!" she accused.

"Honey, if you just think I'm trying, then I'm not doing a good job. I am definitely courting you," he said softly, stepping closer to her.

There was a smell about her that reminded him of springtime. Of new beginnings and hope, of lazy mornings and happiness.

"Well you can just stop courting me right now. You're wasting your time. I'm never going to get married again. Do you hear me?" she asked, her hands on her hips, her eyes bullets in the dark.

"Was your marriage to Thomas so bad?" he asked.

She jerked back, surprised. "No, why would you think that?"

He shrugged. "Maybe because you're so adamant that you'll never marry again. Why Eugenia? Explain it to me so that I can understand."

Whatever had happened in her first marriage, he wanted to make certain that he didn't repeat that same mistake. He wanted a happy home, and if he couldn't have that with Eugenia, he needed to know now.

"Simple," she said. "I don't want to."

"That's hardly an explanation."

"I like my life."

He stepped closer to her, and her sapphire eyes grew larger. She put her hand up to her throat as if to put space between them. "You don't want to get married, but you want everyone around you to be married. If marriage is so important to the people you love, why don't you want it for yourself?"

She tilted her head back and gazed up at him, but for once she didn't say anything.

He stepped even closer, mere inches separating their bodies. She wrapped her shawl tighter around her like a shield. He could see her breath making white wispy clouds in the night air. God, he wanted to kiss her. His body ached with the need to taste her, to sample from her lips.

"I don't know what it is, but there is this thing between us that I didn't feel with Beatrice. This knowing that when we touch, sparks are going to fly." He placed his hands on her arms and drew her to him. She didn't resist.

"I think you're afraid. And you don't want anyone to know that the fearless Eugenia is scared."

"Nonsense," she said, her voice soft and breathless.

"Then prove it to me, Eugenia. Show me you're not afraid of my kiss."

She reached up and hesitantly kissed his lips. He pulled her into his arms and laid his mouth over hers. He kissed her with all the loneliness he'd hidden pouring from his heart onto her lips. He kissed her like a man dying of thirst. He kissed her like he couldn't get enough of her.

After a startled moment, she wrapped her arms around him and clung to him as his lips claimed hers, made her his in every sense. He wanted her to know exactly what she was getting into if she married him. He wanted to leave her panting and restless with desire for him.

Abruptly he broke off the kiss, his body tense and his loins tight. Slowly she opened her eyes, her breathing raspy and her lips swollen.

She pushed away from him and walked deeper into the yard. "Damn it, Wyatt Jones. You had no right to kiss me. You had no right to…"

"You kissed me," he reminded her.

He couldn't restrain his smile. He'd accomplished exactly what he'd wanted. Eugenia Burnett was a woman filled with passion she'd hidden away. He'd hopefully just unlocked her desire and left her wanting.

"Honey, come back here, and I'll soothe that hurt," he promised, his voice low and sensual. He wanted her back in his arms. He wanted a second kiss. A second opportunity to show her the passion between them.

"The hell you will. Go home, Wyatt. Go back to your ranch and leave me alone. I don't want to get married."

She hurried toward the house, almost running, leaving him alone in the yard.

He grinned. Step one accomplished. Eugenia desired him as much as he ached for her. There was a mutual attraction, though she would deny she held any feelings for him.

"'Night, Eugenia," he called. "I'll be looking for your casserole dish."

~

The next morning after church, Eugenia pulled Myrtle Sanders aside.

"Myrtle, did you take a casserole dish out to Wyatt's house?"

The woman stared at Eugenia, confused. She tilted her head, and her hat sat perched at a weird angle. "After what he said to you at the café, I thought there was no sense in me wasting my time. He wants you, Eugenia."

"Well, he understands that I'm not looking for a husband. I think now would be a good time for you to take him your beef noodle casserole." Eugenia needed Wyatt to focus on another woman, any woman but her. She didn't want or need his attention.

"Are you referring to my chicken and rice?"

"Yeah, that's the one," Eugenia said, thinking she didn't care what food the woman took out to Wyatt's house. She just needed her to take a dish so that Wyatt would get the message.

She was still sending him women, and she wasn't interested in marrying him.

Though, God, the man kissed like heaven. All her lady parts had lit up like a firecracker on the Fourth of July. Sleep had been near impossible as she'd tossed and turned, reliving the taste and feel of those lips. Even now she wanted to close her eyes and remember each tiny detail.

But that was impossible. Wyatt was impossible, and she needed to get him married quickly. Before her resolve weakened and she found herself once again taking care of a man and being told when and how to live her life.

Myrtle stood there shaking her head. "I don't think he's interested in me. He barely said hello the other day at the restaurant. It was you that he wanted, Eugenia. You, not me."

Marriage to Thomas had been filled with raising kids and establishing their ranch. But his death had also been liberating. Now her time was her own. Now she did what she wanted, and if anyone didn't like it, then that wasn't her problem.

"Well, I'm not available. Take him a casserole dish. Show him you're interested. Stick to the plan," she said, raising her voice.

People around them glanced in their direction.

"Do you want to remain alone the rest of your life? Or do you want a man in your bed."

"Shh..." Myrtle said, glancing around. "I don't want people to think the wrong thing."

"Well? What do you want?"

"I want a husband."

Eugenia liked her life. She liked being alone. She liked not having a man tell her what to do. Yet Wyatt's kiss had left her sleepless with the need for more. Her body longed to respond to his touch, and her mouth ached with the need for his lips.

Yet, if he were married, he'd be off limits again, just like when he was married to Beatrice. She needed him married.

"Then take Wyatt a casserole," Eugenia said, raising her hands. "A chicken noodle casserole."

"It's chicken and rice."

"Whatever it is. Take it to Wyatt today if possible."

"Okay, but I'm trusting you, Eugenia. I hope he's really interested in me."

"He will be," Eugenia lied, knowing this dish would show Wyatt who had the upper hand. She was not interested in getting married. She was not interested in getting hitched. Still, she couldn't help but think about the way his lips tasted.

She touched her fingers to her lips. The man tasted like sweet, sweet sin.

Chapter Three

Sitting at the kitchen table, Wyatt and Gus finished off the last of the latest casserole dish delivered this afternoon. Gus sat back and rubbed his stomach with his hand. "I think you should marry this one."

But this wasn't Eugenia's casserole. And he was waiting for her to bring him a casserole, proving that she wanted a relationship with him.

Wyatt turned to look at his foreman sitting across from him and raised his brows. "Just because she can cook in the kitchen, doesn't mean her skills in the bedroom are any good."

The memory of his kiss with Eugenia overcame him, spreading warmth through him like the heat from a fire on a cold night. He'd known there was a natural attraction between the two of them, but when their lips had touched, he'd about gone up in flames. He'd been unprepared for the reaction of her mouth beneath his. The sweetness of her lips, the crush of her breasts against his chest, the feel of his arms around her.

"True, but this chicken and rice casserole is so damn good that the bedroom wouldn't matter." Gus all but licked the plate, his fork scrapping across the china.

Wyatt slid his chair back from the table, stood, and stretched. "Hrmp. You've not had great sex in a long time if you think food is better."

"Well, it has been awhile," Gus admitted. "How was dinner with Eugenia's family Saturday night?"

Wyatt laughed. "Great. Eugenia didn't know I was coming, and she wasn't happy to see me."

The look on her face when she'd seen him walk through the door would have sent most men running. She was a fiery woman who presented a tough shield, but he couldn't help but think that once he melted her armor, she'd be soft as a buttercup.

Just the thought of breaking through to that warm, soft woman had his heart racing and his blood rushing.

"Why are you chasing after a woman who doesn't want you?" Gus shook his head at what Wyatt knew he considered outrageous.

But there was a reason to his continued pursuit of a woman who'd turned him down more than once.

"I may be crazy, but I think she does want me. I think she's just resisting, and I don't know why. Once I learn why she's saying no, then she'll soon say yes."

There was a fire in Eugenia that drew him like a clueless moth to an inferno. He knew once he walked into the fire, he'd be consumed, but out of the flames he hoped a happy couple would emerge.

Eugenia was a strong woman who spoke her mind, letting him know exactly where he stood. Yet when he kissed her, all that strength became soft and tender in his arms.

Gus pushed away his plate, lingering at the table. "Is she really going to be worth all this trouble? You've got women banging on the door with casseroles dishes in hand. All you'd have to do is get down on one knee, and any one of them would say yes. How hard is that?"

But Wyatt didn't want just any woman who would have him. He wanted a woman suited to his personality and who would love him unconditionally. He needed a strong personality, like Eugenia.

"Where's the challenge? And once that ring was on their finger, they'd whimper every time I said no. I want a strong-willed woman who is going to agree with me when she thinks I'm right and challenge me when I've done wrong. I want a partner, not a lap dog."

"So you're in this for the chase. Once you've caught her, what are you goin' to do then?"

Ohhhh…he knew exactly what he'd do to Eugenia then. There was no doubt in his mind." Of course I love the chase, but there are qualities in Eugenia you're overlooking. She's a protector, a fighter for the people she loves, and I know when she loves a man, she's beside him to the day he takes his last breath."

"You didn't have that with Beatrice?"

"Beatrice was a great woman. She was strong and independent until she took ill. She loved me, and I loved her until the good Lord took her from me. I need a woman who has spirit, and I know Eugenia has enough stoutheartedness to support an army."

For a moment they sat in silence with Gus contemplating, a frown on his wizened face. They'd been friends for a long time, and the man obviously was troubled by Wyatt's infatuation with Eugenia.

"Eugenia's boys okay with you courting their mama? Two of those boys were once gunslingers. They're a pretty tight bunch. You need to tread lightly with Mama."

Wyatt shook his head, remembering how the family had greeted him with warmth. Even her sons had acted happy to see him. "You're worrying for nothing. I think the daughters-in-law are on my side, and the boys all treated me neighborly at dinner Saturday night. Once Eugenia is purring in my hand, I think the family won't be a problem."

Eugenia had raised her sons to be strong, just like herself, and he admired that in her. For years he'd watched her fight and protect those kids, and he was certain she'd be doing the same for her grandchildren.

"So, did you make progress last night, or was she madder than a hornet that you were there?"

Wyatt smiled at the memory of how he'd left Eugenia. "Oh, I made progress."

"Then why'd we get another widow woman's casserole dish?" Gus asked, his brows drawn together in wrinkled confusion. "If she wanted you, she'd send her own casserole."

"All in good time," Wyatt said, knowing that Eugenia was far from admitting she wanted him. "Eugenia's testing me. And that's all right. I know she'll be in town tomorrow, and I'll return the empty casserole dish."

Wyatt couldn't wait to return the empty casserole dish and let Eugenia know he still wanted her, no one else. He wanted to watch the way her brows would raise on her face, and her luscious mouth would form that perfect O when she realized he wasn't giving up.

"You've got more patience than I would have with that woman. I sure hope you know what you're getting yourself into."

Wyatt smiled. "I do, and this is going to be fun."

~

Sunshine streamed from the cloudless Texas sky, chasing the chill from the air. Eugenia hurried down the wooden sidewalk past the bank, a saloon, and the hat shop toward the mercantile store in downtown Fort Worth. She had to pick up some thread for the baby quilt she was crocheting for Sarah, and then she was going to head over to the restaurant and meet Myrtle for lunch.

She wanted to know how the casserole delivery went. She needed to make certain that Wyatt had gotten the message loud and clear. Stop courting her and focus on another woman that wanted his attention.

As if in a daydream, she saw Wyatt walking toward her, his steps steady and sure, his hat low on his head. He smiled that cocky grin of his, and her heart leaped in response. She glanced at his mouth, remembering the feel of his lips on hers, and immediately knew that to protect her freedom, she needed to get as far from him as she possibly could.

She turned and began to walk as fast as her short legs would carry her in the opposite direction.

And then he was beside her. In little or no time, he'd caught up to her.

"Good morning, Eugenia."

"Wyatt," she responded, surprise ringing in her voice, though she knew she lied.

"Are you avoiding me?" he asked, grinning at her as if he wanted to devour her. And part of her wanted to feel those lush lips of his covering hers again. Why this man?

"Never," she said. Her stomach clenched in a painful knot at the lie. But it was for her own protection.

"Then why did you turn around?"

"I'd forgotten that I needed to go to the feed store," she said, trying to make an excuse.

He threw back his head, laughing, picked up her hand and placed it in the crook of his arm. "The feed store is in the opposite direction.

Drat!

"Wyatt," she hissed. "People will see. They'll think…"

God, why did the touch of his skin make her pulse race like a thoroughbred in the final lengths? And his smell was a combination of leather and soap. A smell that conjured up images of him wet and naked, leaving her breathing a little faster.

"That we're a couple," he responded. "Then they'll be correct."

She glared at him, purposely giving him her stop-what-you're-doing look. "No, we're not a couple. What is it going to take for you to realize I'm serious."

She decided to take a different approach. She stopped in the middle of the street, pulled her hand from his arm, and stared at him. "I'm sorry, Wyatt, but I'm not attracted to you as a man. There could be nothing between us."

He burst out laughing. "Now, Eugenia, don't treat me like I'm a fool." He leaned in close to her and said just low enough for her ears, "I know when a woman is excited, and the kiss we shared the other night would have set the sheets on fire. There is enough attraction between the two of us that we could go without wood for the winter. You're definitely attracted to me."

Eugenia wanted to scream at the man, though his soft-spoken words made her loins begin a slow burn. Instead, she turned and started walking down the street.

"Where are you going?" he asked, hurrying after her.

"To the mercantile," she said, her feet hurrying as fast as she could without running.

"I'll accompany you and then I have to go. Unless you'd like for me to drive you home."

She turned and glared at him. "No."

He smiled, picked up her hand and placed it in the crook of his arm. "You know I enjoy these little skirmishes of ours. Our life together will be interesting."

She raised her brows at him and gave him her best no-nonsense mother look. "If you want to walk me to the mercantile, there'll be no discussion of marriage or our life together."

Her skirts swished, and their boots made a rhythmic sound on the wooden sidewalk. The smell of fresh bread from the bakery wafted through the air, tantalizing with its yeast.

"Would you have dinner with me?"

Oh, he was going to get so tired of hearing her say no that he would soon go away.

"I'm sorry, I'm busy."

"Every night? Every afternoon?"

"I'm afraid so."

He sighed. "You're not going to make this easy are you?"

"Nope," she said, wanting to smile at the frustration she could hear in his voice. "I would suggest Myrtle Sanders. I've heard she bakes a great chicken and noodle casserole, and she's looking for a husband. She's a good woman."

If he wasn't interested in Myrtle, she'd find him someone else. Anyone to get this man married and unavailable.

"It was a chicken and rice casserole. Very tasty, but I'm not interested in her. I find her dull compared to you."

They arrived at the mercantile, and she glanced at him.

He reached into his duffle bag, pulled out an empty casserole dish, and handed it to Eugenia.

"Myrtle Sander's casserole dish." He winked at Eugenia, tipped his hat, and smiled. "Again, it's you I want Eugenia, no one else. No more casseroles unless it's yours."

He turned and walked away, his large frame strolling down the sidewalk as if he didn't have a care in the world while her heart raced, begging her to go after him. Her lips wanted to sip from his again, and her hips wanted to slide against him.

Why couldn't he get the hint? Yet a part of her was doing a little dance inside. If she ever considered marriage again, it would be with Wyatt. But that didn't mean she was ready to accept his advances.

But there was something about the man that reawakened her body, reminding her of the joys of being married. She liked her life. She liked the control she had in doing what she wanted and not listening to any man telling her what to do.

She wouldn't have that if she married Wyatt.

~

Wyatt strode down the sidewalk, tempted to look back and watch Eugenia but refusing to give her the satisfaction. Was he wrong to pursue her? Did she really not want his affections and wasn't attracted to him?

Part of him said to walk away while he still had his pride. While another part of him said to wait. The best was yet to come. Eugenia had her reasons for never wanting to marry again, and he just needed to find out what happened to make her leery of marriage.

Walking down the sidewalk, past the shops and the saloons, he neared the office of Dr. Sarah Burnett. Just as he walked past her door, she came out.

"Mr. Jones," she called. "How nice to see you again."

"Mrs. Burnett. How are you feeling?"

She smiled. "Great for being over eight months along."

"Good to hear," he said, wondering if it would be improper to ask about Eugenia. There was that nagging question of why she didn't want to remarry.

"I just hope he or she isn't born on Christmas," Sarah said.

"Why not?" Wyatt asked, curious.

"I would hate for the baby's birthday to be a holiday. But whenever it decides to arrive is okay with me. I'm ready."

"Babies do come in their own time," Wyatt said, remembering the birth of his daughter and how much he'd wanted more children. Beatrice's health had kept them from having more babies.

Horses and wagons passed them by, the clop, clop, clop of hooves resounding on the hard mud of the street while they stood on the wooden sidewalk in front of her office, chatting like two old friends.

"We were all so glad to have you out to dinner the other night," Sarah said, smiling at him.

"Thank you. I enjoyed myself. Your family seems very close." He had enjoyed the family and Eugenia's company. He could see himself fitting into that group.

"Yes, we're a tight bunch, but there's always room for more. We all enjoyed getting to know you better. And Eugenia came in all flushed from the cold after your stroll."

That flush was caused by her response to his kiss, not the cold. What if they thought he was being too bold? "Eugenia's quite a woman. But I've got a small problem. If you have a moment, could I ask you a question?"

"I'm in no hurry. What's your question?"

Maybe Sarah would tell him the reason Eugenia refused to consider marriage again. Maybe she knew.

"Do you know of any reason Eugenia wouldn't want to marry again? I knew that Thomas was a hard man, but I always thought they had a good marriage."

Sarah smiled. "Tucker says his father was as hardheaded as they come and that he pretty much ruled the house. But Eugenia and he were happy. She was heartbroken after he died."

"Mrs. Eugenia is adamant about not wanting to marry again. I wondered if there was a reason."

Wyatt watched her face carefully to see if he could learn anything new about Eugenia.

"I'm unaware of one. Eugenia wanted her boys happily married. If she didn't believe in marriage, I don't think she would have pushed them the way she did. I'd say just give it some time," Dr. Burnett said, her face open and honest.

"Thank you, Dr. Burnett. I appreciate your time. I'll not give up on her, though I may get fat from all the women and their casserole dishes she's sending my way."

"Another one?"

"Yes ma'am. I brought her back the dish today."

How many more times would he have to experience bringing back a casserole dish because Eugenia wasn't ready to concede there was passion between them?

Sarah laughed. "You're a good man, Mr. Jones."

"Thank you," he said, wondering if he was good or just stubborn.

"You know the church pageant meeting is later this afternoon. Eugenia's always in charge of the children's program. I know she plans to volunteer again, but old Mr. Carter, the previous pageant director, passed away last month. They need a new director. Eugenia works closely with the director."

Wyatt smiled at her and shook his head. "This cowboy a pageant director? I don't think so, ma'am."

He considered what Sarah was saying. He could see Eugenia three times a week whether she wanted him there or not. Of course, she could also quit, but he didn't think so. She was too stubborn to let him win.

"Rehearsals twice a week for the next three weeks. All you have to do is be in charge, make certain they don't go over budget, and help with the auditions. There would be lots of time spent at the church with Eugenia."

"And twenty small children."

Sarah smiled. "There would be that."

"When's the meeting?"

"This afternoon at three."

She'd be mad. Hell, she'd be furious. She'd think he was interfering. It could be a real test to see if they should marry.

"I'll consider it."

The Christmas pageant. He hadn't been involved since his daughter was eight. Now she was grown with a family of her own in Austin, Texas. Little kids, animals, a manger, Christmas, and Eugenia—a show-stopping combination.

"In the meantime, if you have any other questions about Eugenia, come see me."

Wyatt tipped his hat to Sarah. "Take care of yourself and that baby, Dr. Burnett."

She waved and walked on down the sidewalk.

He'd never considered becoming the pageant director, but he would to be near Eugenia. A smile played across his lips. She wouldn't be happy at his nearness. But maybe by the end, she'd want to be by his side.

~

"Thank you for coming," Pastor Brown said to the people gathered in the meeting room of the local Presbyterian church.

The usual parishioners had gathered to volunteer for the Christmas pageant, something Eugenia had led for the last five years. When her husband had passed, she'd needed something to keep her mind off missing him, and she'd gotten involved with the Christmas pageant.

"Mrs. Barnett has agreed to lead the Christmas pageant again this year. Do we have any volunteers to help her?" Pastor Brown asked the few women seated around the table.

Eugenia enjoyed having little kids around, which kept her young, though she wasn't certain how many more years she would lead the pageant. Every year she swore it was her last, and then when the time came around again, she volunteered.

The same women agreed to help her. One for music, one for costumes, and another one that would keep the children focused on where they needed to be at the right time. Eugenia couldn't do it all, and without their help, there would have been mad chaos on stage.

"Who's going to be in charge of the project overall?" Myrtle asked.

About that time the door opened, and Wyatt strolled into the hall, sending her heartbeat into a slow gallop.

What did he want now? Surely he didn't intend to ask her to dinner again. Surely he wasn't here to…

"Sorry I'm late, pastor."

"No problem, Wyatt. I'm just glad you could attend."

Oh no! Oh no! The Christmas carols she'd been considering died in her throat.

Pastor Brown smiled and gazed at the ladies. "Wyatt has offered to be the pageant director this year. He's going to take care of the animals, the funds, and anything else that Eugenia needs help with. Eugenia and Wyatt will work closely to put on our annual Christmas pageant."

The hell they would.

"No," Eugenia said. The word slipped out of her mouth like a bad taste as she cringed inwardly at her gaffe.

"Excuse me, is there a problem Sister Eugenia?" the pastor asked.

How did she get out of this? "I'm sorry. I was thinking out loud and wondering who could play Joseph this year. Our children are all growing up so quickly, and I need someone around the age of ten. Does anyone have any suggestions?"

Wyatt grinned at her, seeming to know exactly what she'd meant when she said no. He touched the tip of his finger to his nose in a silent salute while around them, names were considered for who would play Joseph. Eugenia didn't hear a word they said, her focus entirely on the big man she couldn't seem to escape.

Fifteen minutes later, as they walked out of the church to their separate buggies, Wyatt approached Eugenia.

"Could I escort you home?" he asked, his voice both rough and tender.

How could this man's voice make her insides get all quivery like mush and her lips suddenly dryer than the desert? Why this man?

"Nope," she said, turning her back on him.

"Are you mad?"

"Mad? Whatever would I be upset with you about?" she asked sarcastically, wondering if he'd catch her intonation.

"The fact that I got involved in your pageant?"

She turned and faced him, her hands on her hips. "It's not my pageant. It's the children's pageant. We're supposed to be teaching them about the meaning of Christmas and Christianity. So your being involved is not going to stop me from doing my duty." She walked up to within inches of him. "Don't get in my way, Wyatt. I'm not a woman to be trifled with."

He laughed.

She frowned, realizing that Wyatt laughed a lot, especially around her. She wondered if he'd laugh as much if she quit fighting him and accepted his attentions. He'd always been fun, but she'd never realized how easy he was to be around.

"I'm not going to get in your way. I'm here to help."

"The hell you are. You're here to-to try to court me."

Could no one else around her see what was going on? He was doing everything he could to be in her life, and she wanted him to stop.

He smiled. "I'm just here doing the Lord's work."

"Oh, please. If I hadn't been the pageant coordinator, would you have volunteered for this job?"

He shrugged. "Maybe. I have many interests. When something piques my interest, I'm like a dog chasing a rabbit."

Her brows rose, and she gave him her best I'm-not-believing-you gaze. "Your devious little scheme is not going to work."

"What scheme is that?"

"The scheme to convince me that I should marry you."

"Marriage?" He looked around and shrugged his shoulders. "Who mentioned marriage? I'm here to oversee the Christmas pageant." He tipped his hat. "It's going to be a pleasure working with you, Eugenia."

A part of her wanted to scream at him, throw an absolute fit, but then she knew that would do her no good. And it probably would not make him go away and leave her alone.

She scowled at him. "We'll see about that."

She turned and walked away. She was going to make his life hell as much as she could.

"When is our first rehearsal?" he asked.

"When hell freezes over," she called.

Chapter Four

Chaos reigned in the church auditorium, the hall echoing from the chatter of excited children. Today was audition day with mothers and even a few fathers bringing their children to try for a part in the annual Christmas program.

Since Eugenia had taken on the leadership five years ago, many of the children had grown too old to perform. Now a new set of little ones were involved in the Christmas production. In two years, her grandchildren would be old enough to audition, and she could hardly wait.

"Let's get started," one of her volunteers called out, quieting the crowd.

Eugenia stood before the group, delighted to start the new production. "As you know there are three speaking parts, Mary, Joseph, and a wise man, plus two silent angels and our children's choir. So please line up for tryouts."

She watched her volunteers line everyone up in the right places, and then she sank onto a chair to prepare to listen to twenty auditions.

The door to the auditorium creaked open, and she turned to see Wyatt. Her breathing quickened, and a tingle zipped along her spine as he made his way toward her. The man didn't walk, but rather sauntered. There was a sway about his hips that promised he meant business, and right now his business was her.

He sank down onto the chair beside her and smiled, his lips turned up in a grin that went straight to her heart. Why did his smile warm her better than an overcoat?

"Morning, Eugenia. That color of blue looks very becoming on you." He leaned forward, close to her ear. "It makes your eyes shine bluer than a Texas bluebonnet."

A blush started at her hairline and burned its way across her face. "Stop it, Wyatt. We're in church."

Though she'd meant her voice to sound mean, it came out breathy, as if she'd just run a race trying to escape his flirtation.

She ignored the warm flush his nearness provoked. She ignored the way he smelled of leather and a nice long walk in the woods. She ignored the way her mouth ached to taste his again.

"Why, Eugenia, God loves a man who gives a woman a compliment."

She wanted to roll her eyes at him but refused to give him the satisfaction of knowing how his sweet-talking sassiness left her hotter than the Texas sun.

"Here's a sheet of paper for you to write down thoughts about each kid. When we've heard all of the auditions, we'll compare notes and make a decision." She glanced away from his honey-brown gaze that seemed to start a prairie fire everywhere it touched her.

"Sure, but this is your area of expertise. I'm just here to help."

She frowned. Why was he being so agreeable? Most men wanted to be in charge-taking over, telling her how she wasn't doing it the correct way, and generally treating her like she had rocks for brains. She needed to be very careful. He was luring her in, and then like a cat, he'd pounce and take charge. After all, most men thought they knew best.

"Are you ready to begin?" she asked him.

"Let's get started," he said, his smile melting the ice around her heart. "Maybe afterwards you'll let me buy you a cup of coffee?"

Raising her brows, she stared into his warm-as-Texas golden-brown eyes. "Afterwards I'm having dinner with my son and daughter-in-law."

"Oh. Maybe…"

"We're joining Tucker's friend, Marshal McCoy."

Wyatt shrugged. "Another time."

For a moment she felt a keen sense of disappointment. Ridiculous. She didn't want him to go to dinner with them.

"Another time," she answered, trying to refocus on the children waiting on them.

They would be spending too much time together in the next few weeks. No need to worry. They'd hate one another at the end of the performance. They'd soon be fighting each other for control. He'd soon learn that she was no simpleton and since her first marriage, was now a reformed pushover.

An hour later they both sat there as the last performer auditioned for the day. When he finished, Wyatt turned to her.

"Okay, what's next?"

She stood and gazed at everyone. "If you'll all wait outside, Mr. Jones and I will make our decision and announce this year's lead roles."

After everyone had left the room, Eugenia turned to Wyatt. "Did you have any favorites?"

She just needed to confirm her notes, but she was almost certain of which child she wanted to choose.

"I've already made my choices for Mary, Joseph, the wise men and the angels."

"That was quick. Don't tell me while I make my decision." A few moments later she turned to face him. "Write down your choices on paper, and then we'll turn them over at the same time."

"Okay," he said in that low-voiced drawl that rippled along her spine like tongues of fire dancing across her skin. Now she would see him exercise his control. Now he would tell her which child they should choose. Now she would tell him to go straight to hell, in church.

He wrote his names down.

She looked at him. "Let's flip them over at the same time to see how far apart we are."

"If our names match exactly, then I think I deserve a kiss," he responded, his gaze burning into her.

"You're going to take every opportunity to get a kiss, so listen buckaroo, you're getting nothing."

Though her lips were saying she didn't want a kiss, her mind was remembering, picturing the last time she'd felt his mouth on hers.

"When a man wants a woman, he pursues her, and that's what I'm doing," he said, leaning toward her, his eyes twinkling with laughter.

A warm flush invaded her body like the Calvary coming to the rescue. "You think I should let you kiss me if we match?"

"Why not? Sounds like a good excuse to me."

"We're in church." What if someone walked in and caught them? What if she enjoyed this kiss more than the last one? What if this one pushed her over the edge and right into his arms?

"No place better to smooch than in the house of God."

Eugenia shook her head at him. "This is just an excuse for you."

"Honey, I don't need an excuse to kiss you. I just look for opportunities," he said, his voice low and throaty, sending delicious ripples like miniature waves through her body.

"There's no way we're going to match."

"Then there'll be no reason to kiss you," he said. "Other than I like kissing you."

For some reason his admission warmed her all the way to her toes, and she smiled, feeling like she was sixteen, not almost fifty. "Oh, all right, let's just do this because we're not going to match."

They flipped their papers over, and they both had chosen Timothy for Joseph, Bethany for Mary, Frank for the wise man with the speaking part, Johnny and Junior the other wise men and Ellen and Carolyn for the angels.

Eugenia sat there, stunned, and then she gasped as realization dawned. They'd matched. He would expect a kiss.

"You cheated. There's no way we could have chosen the same people on the first draw. That just doesn't happen."

Speechless she stared at this cowboy and wondered how he had figured out which children she'd chosen?

"Well, it did, and because you accused me of cheating, I'll take two kisses."

She sat back and shook her head, staring at his grin. "That's not possible. Why did you choose those kids?"

"Because I thought they were the most talented and the right age," he said. "Why did you choose these children?"

"They auditioned better, they're the right age, and I've worked with them in the past. I know they'll do a great job."

They'd agreed. Her chest tightened, leaving her a little astounded.

He smiled. "We're in agreement. I think it's the first thing we've ever agreed on except casseroles."

"We're not in agreement on casseroles," she said, still in shock that they had chosen the same children. He'd used the same logic she had and come to the same conclusion.

"No, we're not. You keep sending them. My men are eating them," he said, his brown eyes clearly showing his frustration.

"Glad someone's enjoying the dishes." Eugenia wanted to laugh but didn't. She stood, her feet wanting to move as quickly as possible to the door to avoid what she knew was coming. "I guess we better go announce the winners."

"Not yet," Wyatt said. He stood, and before she could protest, before she could tell him no, he pulled her into his arms. His lips covered hers as his sweet mouth demanded his reward.

His mouth moved over hers, savoring and tasting her as if she were a dish he hungered for, and she couldn't help but let him. This time her brain had longed for this second tasting. This second chance to experience the feel of his mouth on hers, the way he tasted and the gentle way he held her in his arms. The way her body was humming in areas she'd long thought were dead.

His kiss was thorough and tender and created images of the two of them naked, reaching for that ultimate satisfaction.

Somewhere a door slammed.

Eugenia pushed back, her hand coming up to her lips. "Oh my."

She stood there for a moment, trying to regain her bearings, trying to restrain her stampeding heart and regulate her out of control breathing. Finally, she turned to him, straightening her clothing nervously. "We need to tell the others. They're waiting, and we're in here…"

He brushed back a lock of hair from her face. "You look fine, Eugenia. This part of the program was just for us."

He smiled and strolled over to the door and held it open for her. Eugenia stood there trying to get her raging breathing under control, her body thrumming with awareness.

She couldn't remember ever receiving a kiss like that. One that burned all the way from her toes up to the top of her head, leaving scorched places in between.

Finally, he turned to her, a smile on his chiseled, handsome face. "You coming?"

This could not happen. He could not court her. He could not change her mind, and he could not set her aflame like that again.

"Of course, I'm coming," she said with a snap.

Oh my, that man could kiss.

~

Wyatt held the door for Eugenia and watched her flounce through the opening, her long skirt rustling over her petticoats, her taste still on his lips.

He had to restrain his laughter. He couldn't remember when he'd had so much fun chasing a woman. And her resistance made the pursuit even more of a challenge. Sure he wanted her to succumb, but not yet. Not until she was ready to be naked and willing beneath him, because there were enough sparks flying between them to burn the sheets up. Lord, that woman set his limbs afire.

"Everyone gather around," she said, her face flushed from his kiss. "The auditions were outstanding this year. All of you did a great job, but there were five children we thought fit the roles perfectly. The rest of you will still be in the show, but you will either be in the choir or extras."

The kids stood waiting, listening to her attentively. "This year's cast is, Timothy for Joseph, Bethany for Mary, Frank for the speaking wise man, and Ellen and Carolyn as the angels."

The children gave a round of applause and clapped the winners on the back.

"We'll begin rehearsal on Tuesday."

As the kids began to leave, Audelia, mother to Ellen, whiner extraordinaire, approached Eugenia, her ever present frown on her beautiful face.

"Eugenia," she said. "May I have a word with you?"

"Yes, Audelia. How can I help you?"

"My daughter Ruth would have been great as Mary, and yet you put Bethany there. Why did you choose Bethany over her? Ruth is so much prettier and would do such a good job."

Eugenia glanced at Wyatt and raised her brow at him. Wyatt knew better than to fly into that hornet's nest. "I agree Ruth is beautiful, but I needed her voice in the choir leading the younger children who don't know the music as well."

"But that's not fair," she said.

"Ruth is too big to play Mary, and I thought that this year Bethany earned her position in the play," Eugenia told the woman, laying out her reasons for why she'd given each child his part. Seemed reasonable to Wyatt.

Audelia sighed. "I think you're missing an excellent opportunity to have a wonderful production this year. We'll be back for rehearsal on Tuesday."

"Thanks, Audelia. I'll look forward it."

She grabbed her daughter, who stood against the wall, her cheeks red with embarrassment, and led her from the auditorium.

Wyatt walked up beside Eugenia. "Does she think our production is going to New York or San Francisco? It's a church play."

Eugenia shook her head. "Every year it's something with her. Her daughter is a sweet girl, but her mom will drive us crazy before the end of this." She glanced at him. "You certainly didn't step in there and try to explain it to her."

"I'm not here to run the play. I'm here to be supportive and help you. You're in charge," Wyatt said, knowing instinctively that if he'd interfered, Eugenia would have resented his meddling.

She made a harrumph sound. "I'm having a hard time believing that."

He shrugged. "Think what you want. I'm just telling you like it is. I'm here as support."

Why was she having a hard time accepting that he didn't want to lead the play? Could this possibly be a problem with Eugenia? Did she always need to be in control? That could certainly be a problem in any relationship.

~

Sunday morning after the service, Wyatt hurried outside the building. He watched as Eugenia walked over to her family.

"Good morning, Eugenia," Wyatt called.

Outside, people stood in the bright, warm, Texas sunshine waiting for everyone to gather. Buggies were loaded with families as they prepared to ride out in search of a Christmas tree. Every year the church made cutting down the annual tree an outing, except years when the weather had forced them indoors.

"Morning, Wyatt," Eugenia responded.

Wyatt watched as Eugenia walked to her buggy. Beth had laid the bundled up sleeping baby on the bench. There was no place for Eugenia to sit as Rose, Lucas and baby Desirée occupied the front row with Travis. Tanner, Beth, and baby Carter were in the back.

He walked over to their buggy. "Hey there, folks. You guys are a little cramped."

"Good morning, Wyatt," Beth said.

Beth smiled at him, and he knew without a doubt the woman had deliberately put the sleeping baby on the bench.

"Eugenia, baby Carter is sleeping. Why don't you ride with me?"

Her steely blue eyes gazed at him and then back at the sleeping child. She glanced between him and Beth, and he knew she was deliberating whether or not to tell Beth to pick the child up.

Finally, she sighed. "All right, I'll ride with you, Mr. Jones."

She turned and marched to his buggy. He tipped his hat to Beth and smiled. Then hurried to catch up to Eugenia.

He helped her into the wagon, noting the tense line of her jaw, the way her mouth was set in a determined line.

After he climbed up into the buggy, she turned to him. "I don't know how you're doing this or even why you arranged this little buggy ride. But I will talk to Beth and tell her to stop the matchmaking. It's not becoming, and she doesn't know what she's doing."

He pulled the wagon into the line of other wagons all heading the same direction and laughed. He hadn't seen Eugenia since their first rehearsal and then only briefly. He'd missed her quick mind and sharp wit. "That's funny coming from a woman who matched all three of her sons and who's known for her matchmaking."

"Beth's an amateur."

Maybe she was, compared to Eugenia, but she'd helped Wyatt by leaving no room in the buggy for the older Burnett.

"How does it feel, Eugenia?" he asked her, clicking to the horses as they fell into line with all the others. "How does it feel to know that someone is pursuing you and your family has now turned the tables on you?"

She turned and gave him one of her cool, assessing looks.

"Wyatt Jones, you better back off right now, or there's going to be a fight. And I don't play fair."

He laughed, throwing his head back, enjoying riling her so that he could cool her back down. "I love a good challenge. Especially one that will be worth all the trouble to get what I want in the end."

She peered at him, her brows raised in that haughty way that made him want to kiss her and leave her breathless. And, oh God, how he wanted to kiss her.

"Keep on looking at me that way and I will pull this buggy over and kiss you senseless," he said. His eyes strayed to her lips, remembering their feel, their taste, and how he wanted to kiss her again.

"Wyatt! I'm just looking at you. I'm not looking at you with want."

Oh no, her hazel eyes were wide and doe eyed as if all she needed was someone to kiss her, and he wanted to be that someone.

"The hell you aren't. You tell me to my face that you are not interested in me, and I will back off and leave you alone. But your kisses tell me you're not immune to this passion I feel flowing between us, and your eyes are saying come and get me. Tell me, Eugenia. Tell me to go away and I will."

She licked her lips, her eyes suddenly looking wild and confused, like a trapped animal. He almost felt sorry for her. Almost.

"We're working on the Christmas play together. I can't tell you to go away," she insisted.

He shook his head. "Don't use the play as an excuse. You could tell me at any time to walk away if you wanted to, or you could quit the play."

He watched as her body stiffened. "Is that what this is all about? Trying to make me quit so that you can take over the play?"

Deep rolling laughter emanated from within his chest, yet there it was again, her insecurity over him wanting to control the play, when he could care less. Somehow he had to make her understand.

"Honey, I'm only doing this play because it's a place where I can spend time with you. I couldn't care less about this Christmas production. I'm there to make you realize that it's time we faced this attraction that we recognized years ago and refused to act on when we were both married."

She opened her mouth, but no words came out, which was quite extraordinary for Eugenia.

"If you tell me there has never been an attraction between us, I will stop this buggy right now and escort you back to your son and daughter-in-law."

She stared down at her hands and then lifted her steely blue eyes to him.

"Yes, I feel the attraction Wyatt, but I can't act on it."

"Thank you for that admission," he acknowledged. A burst of hope filled his chest, and he no longer felt the biting chill in the wind. "But why can't you act on it? What's stopping you, Eugenia?"

A shout came from the buggy in front of them, and Wyatt knew they'd arrived at the cedar grove right outside of town, where they would cut the church tree and have their picnic. Just when they were finally getting somewhere, they would have to stop and join the others.

He pulled the buggy to a halt and glanced over at Eugenia. She licked her lips nervously and then she faced him, her expression tense and angry as a trapped mama bear.

"I hated being married."

Before he could respond, she jumped out of the buggy and walked away.

Hell-fired! How do I get around that?

Chapter Five

Eugenia watched Wyatt taking his turn at cutting down the large tree they'd found for Christmas. Yes, it wasn't a pine. It was a cedar tree, but in Northwest Texas that was the best they could hope for unless someone took a trip to East Texas.

"Wow, I think he's stronger than Travis," Rose said, stepping up to Eugenia.

Unable to look away, Eugenia perused the way Wyatt swung the ax at the base of the tree. His muscles rippled across his back, his strength showing in the swing of the ax as it struck the cedar.

"Yes, he's strong," Eugenia said, incapable of saying much more as she starred as Wyatt worked.

The man was such a danger to her. Even now, watching him, her body tensed, her breathing quickened, and she seemed to glow when he was around. His quick wit and mind left her wanting to spend more time with him. His kisses were mesmerizing and left her craving things she'd long forgotten.

"He's certainly a good-looking man," Rose said as they stood there watching him cut the tree.

And then that practical voice, the one that reminded Eugenia of how different her life was now and how much she enjoyed being in control of her own destiny, reminded her of her life today. With no one there to tell her how to live each day, with no one demanding her time, with no one limiting what she did.

"Yes, he's not bad looking," Eugenia said, wondering how those muscles would feel beneath her hands. Would his back be strong and taut, his muscles toned? Her stomach tightened at the thought of him naked.

With a shake of her head, she put her hand to her mouth. What was wrong with her to be thinking thoughts like that of Wyatt?

"Some lucky lady is going to make him a fine wife," Rose said softly.

Sure, Eugenia missed the companionship of marriage, but there were so many times Thomas had commanded she do things his way.

"There she goes," Wyatt called to the crowd as the big cedar fell to the ground.

Eugenia's gaze found Wyatt staring at her, his eyes filled with questions. She'd shocked him with her announcement of how she felt about marriage. She'd known it and frankly thought maybe her confession would scare him away.

"There are a lot of good things to consider about the man when you look at Wyatt," Rose commented to Eugenia, her ploy obvious, but Eugenia was entranced staring at Wyatt.

"Yes," Eugenia said, only half listening to Rose.

His eyes gleamed, and as he stood there breathing hard, leaning on the ax handle, somehow Eugenia knew without a doubt that she'd only intrigued him with her confession.

Wyatt strode over to help the men lift the tree and gently lay it in the back of the wagon. He stepped behind the group of men and watched as they tied the tree down for the return trip to town.

His gaze met hers across the space, his eyes warm, the look sending a trail of heat down her spine as she returned his stare, feeling so confused as to what she wanted.

"He certainly watches you," Rose said, glancing back and forth between the two of them.

"Uh-huh," Eugenia replied, refusing to say more.

"I heard he stood by his wife right up until the day she died," Rose said, holding Desirée's hand as the little one tried to toddle off.

"Yes, he did. Beatrice was a friend of mine. Thomas and I had dinner at their house several times." Eugenia still scrutinized Wyatt as he helped the men pack away the tools.

Rose gazed at Eugenia. "He's a good man."

"You're right. He is a good man," she said, her voice barely a whisper. She needed to get away. She needed to quit watching this man. "And you're being way too obvious. I need to unpack our food."

Eugenia walked away, not wanting to talk any longer about Wyatt. Needing to escape the ring linking her to Wyatt growing tighter and tighter.

A few minutes later, dinner was served buffet-style from the back of one of the wagons. Everyone had contributed something, with several serving fried chicken, sliced ham, and potato salad in addition to all the pies anyone could ever dream of in one location.

Women spread blankets on the ground for their families to sit on while the children scampered around in the chilly December air.

A picnic in December was rare, but the Texas sun blazed down on them, giving them a wonderful, toasty day. Not unheard of for December, but still a rarity.

Wyatt walked towards Eugenia carrying two plates of food. "Have you eaten yet?"

"No," she said, and her heart warmed at the sight of him and at his thoughtfulness. She'd been watching her grandson kick a ball with some of the other children and had yet to get in line.

"I brought you a plate. I thought maybe we could sit on the back of my wagon. I pulled it over close to Travis and

Rose," he said, his gaze sizzling and inviting, giving her pause to consider his request.

"Thanks," she said, wanting to refuse, but unable to decline his company.

Eugenia took a seat on the tailgate of his wagon and stared across the blanket at her children. Sarah had stayed home with Kira, the young Chinese girl she'd rescued, by her side. At eight months pregnant, she'd chosen not to attend the tree cutting, but Tucker had brought Lucas. Tanner and Beth were there with baby Carter and then Rose, Travis, and Desirée.

She loved her children, their wives, and her grandchildren more than her next breath, and she knew that because of her marriage to Thomas, they were in her life.

Eugenia glanced at Wyatt. He sat watching her, looking at her with such an intent gaze.

"Oh, go ahead and say it," she said. "You're shocked I hated being married."

Living with Thomas was hard, and when he passed away, she'd grieved. Their marriage had been a sturdy rock, a firm foundation that they'd built their family and ranch on. The years had been good, but now she realized she needed more than a bossy man.

Wyatt continued chewing his food, glancing out at her children and their families. "Nice looking family you have, Eugenia."

She just didn't know if she could do that again with another man. She just didn't know if she wanted another man giving her directions. She just didn't know if she wanted to give her heart to another man to have him leave her to grieve again.

Eugenia let her fork drop onto her plate. "You're not going to say anything about what I told you this morning?"

He turned his attention back to her, his cinnamon eyes twinkling, the corner of his mouth turned up in that sassy-sexy grin that made her want to kiss it away. "It's hardly the time or the place to discuss this matter."

She drew her brows together. "Why?"

"And after I thought about it, why should I be shocked? It's obvious you're resisting every attempt I make," he said, not gazing at her, but down at his plate. "Did you try that chicken salad? That's really good."

Was he deliberately acting nonchalant about her revelation this morning just to goad her into confessing?

"It's Mary Eugene's recipe," she said. "Are you ready to give up pursuing me?"

Her heart did a little stutter step, and she realized she didn't want him to give up. But she didn't want marriage. What did she want?

He smiled. "No, but sooner or later you're going to have to tell me why. Ride back with me, Eugenia."

Part of her wanted to beg off, but another part of her wanted him to understand. Needed him to understand her reasoning for why she didn't want him to pursue her.

"Yes," she finally said, not knowing for certain that she'd made a wise choice, but knowing Wyatt was a special man. He deserved to know why she kept saying no.

"We could leave the picnic right now, but I fear the speculation we'd create," he said. "Not that I care, but you might."

"No. I don't want to stir up speculation."

The tongues would already be a wagging since she was sitting next to him and they were working on the Christmas pageant together.

Wyatt smiled at her. "God, you know how to use a man's words against him."

She shrugged. "It's the truth."

Lucas came running up, his shirt pulled out of his pants, his face red from exertion. His sweet baby face already disappearing into a little boy's features. "You promised to teach me horseshoes."

"Did someone set up a game?" Wyatt asked the boy.

He reached out his hand. "Yes, come and show me."

Wyatt set his plate down, took the boy's hand, and stood up from the wagon. "Excuse me, Eugenia. Lucas and I are going to play horseshoes."

Eugenia watched the pair walk away. He was good with her grandchildren. Her family liked him, and no matter what obstacle she threw at him, he wouldn't let it deter him from his pursuit of her. But she had to stop this before it went any further.

She had to stop this before someone got hurt. She had to stop this before she got hurt.

~

As the afternoon sun slid down the western sky and the temperatures started to cool, the crowd began to pack up their buggies for the drive back to town.

When Wyatt and Lucas finished playing horseshoes, he brought the boy back to Eugenia. He was looking forward to a lively conversation on the return trip about why she didn't like marriage. He was anxious to hear her reasoning.

He walked around the twenty or more buggies, searching for her dark hair spun with gray. Her sweet voice with its southern drawl that made him smile. As he strolled along, he saw her, seated in her son's wagon with baby Desirée in her lap.

His breath tightened in his chest. What was it about Eugenia that had his body responding to the sight of her? Why did he want to spend so much time with her?

He strode toward them, and when he came up on their wagon, she gazed at him, her blue eyes challenging him. He lifted Lucas up into the wagon beside his grandma.

"Wyatt, I need to ride home with Travis and Rose. Desirée is getting fussy, and one of us has to hold her all the time."

Rose climbed into the wagon. "You can hand her to me now, Eugenia."

Looking directly into Eugenia's sapphire eyes, he smiled, knowing she had just been caught in a lie. Eugenia sat there frowning, but finally released the child to her mother, and Wyatt decided to make it easy on her.

"I'll see you at rehearsal on Tuesday," he said, wondering how much longer he could continue this game with Eugenia. Frustration gripped his insides and twisted them tighter than a vise.

Time was running out before he quit chasing this woman who he knew was attracted to him but held back. God, whatever Thomas had done to her, it was hell trying to get her to consider marriage again.

"I'll see you then," she responded.

He turned and walked away, realizing that somehow she'd had second thoughts about telling him why she hated marriage. Every time he thought they'd made progress, she took a step back. How much longer could they do this?

～

Tired, Eugenia sat on the edge of the buggy with Lucas between her and Rose. He leaned his head against her shoulder.

"Nana, why aren't you married?" Lucas asked.

"Because your grandfather passed away before you were born," Eugenia said, thinking this was a new question he'd yet to ask her.

"Passed away?"

"He died."

Lucas sat up, gazing at her with eyes so much like his father's that she wondered how Sarah had kept his paternity a secret for so long.

"Don't you want to get married again?" he questioned, his sweet little-boy face gazing at her in wonder.

"Not really."

He frowned. "Wyatt showed me how to play horseshoes this afternoon. I like him."

"Good. I'm glad."

"He needs a wife," the boy said, tugging on her dress sleeve to make certain she heard him.

Eugenia turned to look at her grandson, knowing instinctively what was about to come out of this babe's mouth, wondering where he'd heard this statement.

"I told him he should marry my nana."

"And what did he say?" she asked, thinking of ways that she could do bodily harm to Wyatt.

"He told me he would ask you."

Eugenia took a deep breath to calm the anger exploding within her. Her blood began to writhe and roil like a serpent in search of its victim. She wanted to wring his neck for bringing her grandson into this. Wyatt had no right to persuade her grandson that she needed a husband.

"Please say yes, Nana," the child whined.

A calmness she'd forgotten she possessed soothed her frazzled brain. "Lucas, marriage is not something that people enter into lightly. You should love the person that you marry."

"But Momma says we're supposed to love everyone. Don't you love Wyatt?" he asked.

Oh, the innocent questions of children. "Yes, we are to love everyone, but love between a man and a woman is a different kind of love."

"How?"

Eugenia was going to beat Wyatt. She was going to tie him up and whip him with a switch! How did someone explain to a five-year-old the difference in the love between a man and a woman?

"You love me, right?"

"Yes."

"You love Momma and Daddy and this new baby that's coming, right?"

"Yes. But your momma and daddy, they love different from the way they love everyone else." Eugenia said, hoping that Lucas wouldn't say something completely inappropriate.

Lucas made a face. "Yeah, they like to kiss."

"Exactly. You don't go around kissing everyone, do you?" she asked innocently, still wishing bodily harm on Wyatt.

"No."

"That's the difference between a husband and a wife's love. They like to kiss," Eugenia said, hoping that was his last question. Almost certain of what he would ask next.

"So you don't want to kiss Wyatt?"

Eugenia took a deep breath and ignored the snickers coming from the front of the wagon. How did she answer that? She did enjoy the feel of Wyatt's kiss, but she couldn't say that out loud in front of her kids and grandkids. She would never admit to them that the man's lips made her feel like a young woman. She would never admit the feel of his lips left her hungry for more.

"No, Lucas, I don't want to kiss Wyatt," she said firmly. No, at this moment, she didn't want to kiss Wyatt. She wanted to torture him slowly for making her lie to her grandson.

"I guess this mean you're not going to marry him," Lucas said with a pout. "I was hoping he would be my new grandpa."

More snickers came from up front, and if she could be certain it wouldn't shame Lucas, she would have hit each of her sons over their heads.

"Lucas, I never intend to marry again."

Eugenia clenched her fists, the hair on the back of her neck standing at attention. Never involve her grandchildren if a man wanted to court her. That was a little too close to home, and she would die fighting for her kids and grandkids. Never mess with her family unless a person wanted to get hurt.

Wyatt was about to get hurt. She would go out and tell him to back off completely. Involving her grandson made it clear. It was time to end this now.

~

Wyatt heard his hounds braying and the sound of a buggy coming into his yard. He peeked out the window in time to see Eugenia pull up to the hitching post. He opened the door and stepped on the porch. "Eugenia?"

"We need to talk."

There was that tone back in her voice that told him she wasn't there on a social call.

He shooed the dogs away and helped her alight from the buggy.

"Come on in," he said.

"No. I can't. That wouldn't be proper. And this won't take long."

He smiled and reached for her hand. She pulled away. Something had made her mad enough that whoever stepped into her path today was bound to get stung.

"Do you want to sit on the swing?" he said, pointing to the swing he'd built Beatrice on the porch.

"No," she said, cutting him off and taking a step back from him. "Did you talk to my grandson about us yesterday?"

Wyatt looked stunned for a moment. "No, he asked me some questions."

"You didn't tell him that you were going to ask me to marry you?" she asked, her sapphire eyes flashing at him.

Wyatt shrugged. "He asked me if I had a wife. I told him no, so then he offered you up to be my wife. What could I do? If I said no, then the boy would think that I didn't like you or I was lying to him. So I said yes, I would ask you to marry me."

An innocent conversation would now be strung up, and Wyatt might as well swing from a rope because at the end of the day, she would still be mad enough she'd think he did this on purpose.

"I had to explain to him on the ride home why I could never marry you," she said with a rush. "I had to tell this sweet child that I never intended to marry another man," Eugenia said, her body tense.

Wyatt took a deep breath and tried to calm her down. "I'm sorry. It was an innocent conversation. I had no idea where it was going until he started asking me to ask you to marry me," he said. Then leaned over and whispered. "You should have ridden home with me."

It was the wrong thing to say. Eugenia bristled like a porcupine ready for battle.

She stepped closer to him, her blue eyes flashing with enough heat to set the prairie afire. "I don't need you, Wyatt. You have managed to finagle your way into my family. You have convinced my children that I would be better off with you by my side." Her voice rose. "But I have no intentions on ever marrying again."

Wyatt reached out and pulled her to him. His lips covered hers, his mouth greedily drinking from her mouth. He held her until he felt her body relax, her mouth opening for him to plunder.

His mouth effectively shut her up. He was tired of her protests. He was tired of her refusing him. He wanted her willing and wanting.

She pushed away from him. "What in the hell do you think you're doing? I'm trying to put a stop to this, and you're kissing me."

He wanted to laugh, but she was riled up madder than a bantam rooster at a cockfight. He took a deep breath and released it slowly. The time was upon them to either make hay or go their separate ways.

"If it's over because your grandson is smart enough to see the attraction that you're denying, then I wanted to end it properly. I wanted to give you a send-off that will hopefully keep you awake at night," he said, his voice lowering. "I want you to miss me."

Her brows drew together in a frown, and she stared at him. "I like my life. I don't need a husband."

He touched the rim of his hat with his fingers. "Okay, then like I said, I wanted to give you a proper send-off."

She crawled back up in her wagon.

"I'll see you Tuesday, Eugenia."

She gave him a quizzical glance. "At rehearsal?"

"Yes, rehearsal."

She hesitated. Finally she turned the wagon around, and Wyatt watched it roll out of the gate.

Damned woman refused to recognize the attraction between them. He didn't want to give up, but what else could he do?

If they were going any further, she had to come to him.

~

As Eugenia urged the horses through Wyatt's gate, she took a deep breath and sighed. That had certainly gone well. Hadn't it? He'd agreed with her, and she'd believed him right up until the moment he kissed her.

Then the doubts overwhelmed her. Was she doing the right thing? Was her grandson right, and she should really consider Wyatt? Was he like her previous husband and had to control everything?

Still, so far he'd remained in the background for the Christmas pageant.

The man had so many good qualities about him that she liked, but she didn't want to get married again. She didn't want to be under the control of a man again.

So, why was she leaving with her chest aching and her heart bruised and battered? Why was she suddenly doubting her decision?

She needed Wyatt to be unavailable. She had to find him another woman. A lucky woman who wanted to marry. A woman who would make him happy. A woman who would put him out of reach for Eugenia.

She slapped the reins against the horses back and headed the wagon into town to Myrtle's house. Now there was a woman looking to find a man.

~

The next day, Wyatt heard a timid knocking, and for a moment he hoped it was Eugenia returning, though he doubted she'd be out again.

He opened the door and there stood Myrtle Sanders, her hands shaking, holding a covered dish. He took a deep breath, exhaled slowly. Damn Eugenia was up to it again.

"Good morning, Myrtle. How are you today?"

She bit her lip nervously and handed him the casserole dish. "Here. I don't think for a moment that you're interested in me, but Eugenia told me to bring you this dish. She said you'd know what it meant."

He took the ceramic pan from her. "Thank you, Myrtle. Can I invite you in for a cup of tea or coffee?"

"Oh no. I just wanted to do what Eugenia asked me and bring you the casserole."

Myrtle delivering a casserole dish meant Eugenia was back to finding him a woman. Someone she could handpick and make him unavailable. What if he gave her what she wanted? What if he asked Myrtle to help him?

"Myrtle, I know the men and I will enjoy this very much. Thank you. But when Eugenia asks you how the meeting went, would you do me a favor? Would you tell her that you and I are having lunch Sunday after church? Don't misunderstand me, you're a lovely woman, but I think it's time Eugenia needs to realize that what she's doing could be hurtful to those of us who care about other people."

For a moment he thought he'd gone too far. She considered his words, and then she smiled.

"Wyatt, you care about Eugenia, don't you?"

"Yes, and she refuses to admit she cares about me. I think she does, but she won't let me close enough to know," he admitted. "You would be helping me out."

She laughed. "Eugenia deserves this. She's sent me out here twice, and both times I told her you weren't interested in me."

Wyatt held his breath, hoping she'd help him.

"I'd love to have lunch with you tomorrow, Wyatt. It will be our one and only special date."

He breathed a sigh of relief and felt his muscles relax. He was back in the game. He was back in the hunt. He smiled at her. "Thank you, Myrtle."

"Well, I better get back. After church tomorrow, I'll walk out with you, and then we can have lunch together."

Wyatt laughed. "Thanks, Myrtle, and my men really enjoyed your dish the last time. I'll bring back the pan tomorrow and hand it to you directly."

She smiled. "See you tomorrow, Wyatt."

~

Gus looked at the casserole dish that Wyatt sat in front of him that evening in the house.

"Oh no, another casserole," Gus said, throwing his hands up in the air. "Is this Eugenia's?"

Wyatt sighed. "No."

"Good God almighty, she's still sending you women, and you're still pining like a lily-livered sapsucker for her," his ranch foreman said, gazing at him like he was the biggest fool this side of the Red River. Maybe he was.

"No, I'm not," Wyatt said.

"Then why such a face?"

"I have a plan."

"Another one. It's not like the last four or five have worked. How is this one going to be different?" Gus asked, leaning back in his chair to look at Wyatt.

"Myrtle has agreed to be my pretend date at lunch this Sunday at the café," Wyatt said, not knowing if what he was doing would work or just drive a further wedge between him and Eugenia. Any chance of the two of them being together was running out of time. This was their last opportunity.

"And Myrtle knows you're just using her to get even with Eugenia?"

"She agreed."

Gus shook his head and laughed. "I think I'll go to the café on Sunday just so I can witness this touching scene."

Wyatt shrugged. "Show up. I have nothing to hide."

"When are you going to give up on this woman? If she wanted you, don't you think the two of you would be finding a preacher man?"

They weren't ready for a preacher man. Not until Eugenia made the decision to come to him willing. She had to agree to let him court her before they could ever marry.

"Sometimes things are complicated, Gus. I know she wants me. I'm certain she will come to love me."

But he wasn't quite as certain as before. There was still this deep, burning passion that seemed to cloak and envelop them, but this was his last attempt. If this didn't work, he was done.

Gus shook his head. "What makes you so certain?"

"Because when we kissed—"

"You kissed Eugenia Burnett?"

Wyatt smiled. "It's usually what you do with a woman you're attracted to. You start off kissing, and then later, much later, it builds to something more."

Those kisses were what sustained him. If those kisses weren't real, then nothing he'd ever believed about love was true.

Gus started laughing. "Wow, I never thought she'd let you kiss her."

"You know, Gus, how when Beatrice used to bake those apple-cinnamon pies you loved, you'd go in the kitchen and you'd smell the aroma of the pie, and you couldn't wait to taste it just as soon as it came out of the oven? You'd savor the thought of that pie all day."

Eugenia would either be the best apple pie he'd ever experienced, or Wyatt would find himself eating crow. One of the two.

"So Eugenia smells like apple pie."

"No. But it's the anticipation. It's the chase, the thrill of the hunt. The knowing that when she gives in, it could be the best apple pie I've ever tasted."

"And what if she doesn't give in?"

"Then you're stuck with me telling you stories of Beatrice's apple pies and how wonderful they were."

Gus picked up the spoon and filled his plate with the casserole. He took a bite, and Wyatt watched him lick his lips and take a second bite. "Damn, this is good. Forget Eugenia and marry Myrtle."

Wyatt took a bite of the casserole. "That woman can cook."

"We don't even know what Eugenia's cooking tastes like. She could be a terrible cook."

"Her cooking skills don't matter." Hopefully tomorrow at church, Myrtle and he together would motivate Eugenia, make her see that she was denying them a chance. If not, it was time to move on.

~

Sunday morning after the church service, Eugenia glanced around the congregation looking for Myrtle. She had to know if she'd delivered the casserole to Wyatt. As she looked toward the doorway of the church, she saw them.

For a moment her stomach plummeted, and her heart started galloping faster than a wild stallion as she watched Wyatt hand over an empty casserole dish to Myrtle. She smiled up at him, and he seemed to thank her for the dish. She turned her back to Eugenia and took Wyatt by the arm, and then the two of them strolled from the church.

Eugenia sank down on the nearest bench. Her chest squeezed painfully tight, and tears pricked her eyelids.

What was wrong with her? This was exactly what she wanted. She didn't want Wyatt in her life. She didn't need him. She'd said so over and over.

Yet there she was wanting to blubber on like a heartsick calf, crying out in distress because she'd matched up Myrtle and Wyatt.

"Mom, you okay?" Travis asked. "Rose is ready to go. I think we're going to go to the café for lunch."

For a moment, she sat there as the realization came to her that she'd been enjoying Wyatt's flirtation. She'd been enjoying his attention. She'd miss his kisses.

"Huh?" Eugenia said as she stared up at her son. He looked so much like his father that she often thought it was Thomas she was staring at.

"Lunch. We're going to go to the café. Are you all right?"

She glanced at the entryway of the church, happy to see that Wyatt and Myrtle had moved out the door. There was no reason for her to be upset. They'd only done what she set in motion. She'd given up Wyatt Jones to another woman because of her own stupid pride.

"Mom!" Travis said again, this time more urgently.

She waved her hand at him. "I'm fine."

"Well, you're not acting like yourself, or maybe you are."

"What's that supposed to mean?"

"It means can we please go so that I can take Rose and the baby to the café," he said, putting his hands on his hips.

"I can't go to that café," she said adamantly.

"Then you're going to have to wait outside, because I'm taking my wife and daughter out to lunch," Travis said, staring at her as if she were going senile.

Eugenia grimaced. It wasn't often that he took them to lunch at the café, but she was so afraid she'd find Wyatt there with Myrtle.

"All right, let's go. But if Wyatt…"

Travis held up his hand. "Unlike my mother, I refuse to play matchmaker, so I don't want to hear your Wyatt stories."

A few minutes later, Travis led them into the café with Rose following him, the baby in her arms, and Eugenia behind the two of them. She glanced around the café, hoping not to see Wyatt and Myrtle, but there they were like a man and wife sitting together at a table.

"Mom, come on. They're seating us."

She held her head high, her back ramrod stiff as she walked through the restaurant until she heard her name.

"Eugenia."

Dear God, Myrtle was calling out to her? Myrtle, who probably thought she'd snagged the hottest man in town. She turned toward her and played like she'd just seen them.

"Myrtle, I missed you at church this morning. And Wyatt. Look at you and Myrtle."

"Eugenia," he responded, his eyes barely meeting her gaze.

"How was the casserole?" she asked directly at Wyatt.

"Delicious," he said, his honey-brown eyes staring at her and sending daggers into her bruised heart.

What had she done?

"Good. I always knew Myrtle was a great cook. Well, I best be going. The family is waiting for me. See you at rehearsals on Tuesday."

"See you then," he said.

"I'll talk to you later, Myrtle," Eugenia said and walked away from the table, her stomach clenching tighter than any cinch she'd ever used on a horse. If she made it to the table without throwing up, it would be a miracle.

What had happened? When had she begun to care for Wyatt? She didn't want another woman sending Wyatt casserole dishes.

Oh God, what did she do now?

Chapter Six

Eugenia hurried from the cold into the crowded church hall. The first blue norther of the season had blown in, reminding them it was winter in Texas. Before now, the weather had been warm enough that a lightweight shawl would suffice, but no longer.

She hung up her coat and watched as the children, already gathered into their perspective groups, practiced. She could hear the choir rehearsing the songs they would sing and the three wise men acting like boys in the corner.

Wyatt came around the corner with his arms loaded down with firewood. "Afternoon, Eugenia."

"Afternoon, Wyatt. Thanks for filling up the wood box for us," she said, her heart contracting at the sight of him.

Gazing at him, she felt such a fool. Such an idiot to have let Myrtle have him. But until there was a ring on the widow Sanders's finger, he was still fair game.

"Least I could do. How else do you need me to help out?"

She glanced around and noticed her wise men were acting foolish in the corner. "Could you work with the wise men tonight? Go over Frank's lines and make certain the others know when to come in.."

He nodded. "As soon as I get the stove fired up, we'll get started."

He headed over to the wood box in the corner and dumped his load of wood. The man was still as strong as an ox, his muscles clearly defined even through his shirt.

She walked over to the children playing Mary and Joseph. "Okay, let's get started so we can get out of here at a decent hour."

Audelia Bryant walked over to Wyatt. "Mr. Jones, I need to speak with you."

"Go ahead," Wyatt said, standing up after filling the wood stove with logs to keep the room warm.

"My daughter Ruth should be playing Mary, not Bethany. She's talented and beautiful. I'm appealing to you make this a better play."

Eugenia felt the hair on the back of her neck rise to attention. She took a deep breath, determined not to react to this overbearing mother. The woman knew they were in the same room and could hear every word each other said. She was deliberately causing trouble. How Eugenia reacted would be taken home by the children to their families and repeated over and over. She'd learned after the first year to never say anything she didn't want repeated around these children.

Wyatt smiled at Audelia. "I'm here at the request of the committee to oversee the production financially. I make none of the cast decisions. Those are handled by Eugenia. I can only refer you to her."

"Fine," she said and walked away.

Eugenia watched as Wyatt turned and smiled in her direction. He touched the tip of his finger to his nose in that silent salute he often gave her, and she smiled, her nerves dancing down her spine in tune with "O Holy Night."

Even Ben Carter, the previous man in Wyatt's position, had never given her this much control. Wyatt seemed to tell everyone she was in charge, acting as if he was only there to help and pay the bills.

Warmth spread through her, chasing away the chills, and she couldn't keep from smiling. Wyatt let her have control, never forcing his opinion or suggestions down her throat until she wanted to choke, like so many men were apt to do.

Could he be different from Thomas? Could he be less demanding and controlling?

Bethany tugged on her skirt. "Are we going to practice today?"

She shook her head. "You're right. Let's get started. I want to hear your parts."

The children began to say their parts, and Eugenia tried to concentrate, but images of Wyatt plagued her.

Beatrice, Wyatt's deceased wife, had been her friend. She'd had the usual complaints about her husband—he left his clothes on the floor, didn't pick up after himself—but she'd never said anything that Eugenia could remember about him being controlling.

The children had finished their lines and were staring at her expectantly.

"Let me hear you say the lines again," she said, knowing her mind wasn't listening.

Their daughter had grown up, married, and moved before her mother passed away, and she knew that Wyatt went to see her a couple of times a year.

They were both alone. They were both family oriented. They were both stubborn, and there was that spark that when he touched her, her lady parts sang three-part harmony.

While the children said their parts to her, she couldn't help but watch Wyatt as he practiced with the wise men.

"Mrs. Burnett, did we do okay?" Timothy asked.

She glanced around. "Yes, yes, you did fine. Let's try again."

He was a good man. Would she let him slip away from her without exploring what a relationship with Wyatt would be like? What if marriage to Wyatt would be different from that with Thomas? What if marriage to Wyatt was exactly what she'd hoped for so many years ago? What if Wyatt loved her even more deeply than Thomas had?

~

When the last child ran out the door to meet his parent, Wyatt was alone with Eugenia for the first time in days.

He watched her putting on her coat and hat. "Are you going to be okay getting home? It's almost dark."

Eugenia laid her hand on his arm and turned her sapphire eyes on him as she smiled. "I'm just going to Tucker and Sarah's tonight. I'm not driving back to the ranch."

"Good. Is your buggy outside?" he asked, wondering if he should drive her home and then come back.

"No. I walked over," she said. "The girls and I are doing some Christmas preparations tomorrow just in case the baby decides to arrive early. We're spending the day together in town, so I thought I'd stay the night."

"Would you let me escort you to your son's house?" he asked, wanting to see her home safely but also interested in checking out her temperature since the Myrtle lunch.

She'd said nothing, but yet she seemed more responsive to him.

"Thank you, Wyatt. I'd appreciate that." She smiled at him in a way he hadn't seen since that first time he'd returned all those casserole dishes.

He held the door open for her as they left the church. He thought about picking up her hand, but before he could make the move, she slipped her gloved fingers into the crook of his arm. She smiled at him, and he noticed the way her eyes twinkled with merriment.

The cold air whipped around the buildings, causing her to shiver. "I think winter has arrived."

"It does seem to look that way," he said. Why did she seem more receptive tonight? Whatever the reason, he wasn't going to push his luck. He liked it when they were relaxed and at ease with one another.

"I have to thank you for standing up for me today. This is twice now you've told a parent that I'm in charge of the Christmas program. Thank you."

He shrugged. "Nothing that needs a thank you. You are in charge of the Christmas program. I'm just here to help you."

She looked at him, her eyes puzzled. "Why aren't you trying to take control?"

With sudden clarity he realized that Eugenia needed to feel in charge. This pageant was hers, and if he'd even tried to suggest any changes, she probably would have shown him the door. Was this her problem with marriage?

Their heels made clomp, clomp, clomping noises on the wooden sidewalk as they walked past the hotel into the heart of the city. He stared at her, wondering where that question came from.

"Why do you think I want control? Do you think I know anything about how to get these kids to perform on stage without making an ass of me?" he asked.

She shrugged. "Most men like to be in charge."

"Hell, I could barely get my wise men to read their parts tonight. Johnny was too busy making rude noises while Frank was trying to read his part, and Junior kept making goo-goo eyes at Ellen. I don't know how you do this year after year." He watched the lights of dusk shimmer in her gaze, and he wondered if they had made any progress or were still sitting at the starting gate.

Eugenia laughed, the sound a tinkling noise in the night air. "You have to smile at them and say, 'You have a choice—you can practice, or I'll find another kid to take your place.'"

She was laughing with him. She was smiling, and they were having fun together, and when he reassured her she was in charge, she relaxed.

"I'll remember that the next time I'm working with them," he said, snuggling into Eugenia. "Why do you think I would want control of this circus act?"

Eugenia sighed and glanced up at the stars in the night sky. "A lot of men think that women don't have a lick of sense and can't get out of the rain without their help. I've never been that type of woman, and I resent being treated that way."

"Have I ever treated you like that?"

She stared, considering him. "No, you haven't."

"Women are soft where men are hard, but I know from watching Beatrice that she could motivate people better than me."

"Yes, Beatrice was good like that."

"So did you truly believe I was trying to take over your Christmas pageant?" he asked, smiling down into her shimmering blue eyes, wanting to get lost in her gaze, knowing not now, not yet.

"I didn't know. But I thought you would tell me how to run it since I'm just a poor little woman who needs guidance." She fluttered her eyelashes at him.

Wyatt threw back his head and laughed out loud in the cold night air. He enjoyed this Eugenia. This was the woman he wanted to marry.

"I feel sorry for any man who believes that about you. Once you got ahold of them, they would be sitting a little shorter in the saddle."

Eugenia laughed. "Well, it's true."

Wyatt stopped on the wooden sidewalk and turned toward Eugenia, wanting to kiss her, but still holding back. "I think you're a smart woman who has done the Christmas pageant for enough years to know what she's doing. You don't really need me, but it makes me feel good to be there helping you."

Her mouth fell open in shock, and he could see her contemplating everything he'd just said. He was tempted to kiss that open mouth, but before he went any further, he needed to know that she wanted him to pursue her. He was done pursing a woman who didn't want his attention.

Myrtle's casserole dish still hung between them.

He turned, and they walked down the sidewalk again, and this time she was quiet as they strolled along.

"So how are the wise men doing?" she finally asked.

"I think we should rename them the wise-ass boys. Because how these three are ever going to pull off offering frankincense and myrrh to the baby Jesus is beyond me."

She chuckled. "Did you hear the choir tonight? I think they finally have "O Holy Night" down."

"Yeah, now only three more songs to learn," he said. "You know I may never ever be able to listen to this music again."

"Give it a month. It will finally leave your head," she said.

"It's hard to believe that Christmas is only one week away."

"It's hard to believe we've already been rehearsing for two weeks, and they're not any further along," Wyatt said, wondering how she would manage to get the children ready.

"Give them time. It will come."

"Now see here, this is why you're program director and I'm just over the finance. I would have already run out of the building screaming."

She laughed. "We're at my door."

"Yes, we are."

God, he wanted to kiss her good-night, but he wasn't making another first move. This time it was up to her.

"Wyatt, I owe you an apology. My grandson had no idea what he was saying or even what the concept of marriage is at his age. I should never have come to your place in such a snit."

"Why thank you, Eugenia. It was innocent on your grandson's and my part." She was apologizing, and it gave him hope. Maybe there was still a chance for them.

She smiled. "Yes, I believe it was. Though my grown kids got quite a chuckle hearing me explain the different kinds of love to him."

Wyatt smiled and wondered if they'd somehow turned a corner. If somehow she would give him permission to court her. But he was not going to bring it up. He'd gone to the line, and now it was her turn.

"At least you explained love to him. A life without love would be rather bleak, don't you think?"

She gazed at him. "Wyatt, you surprise me at every turn. I would never expect a man to have such a conscious understanding of love."

"It's true. When you lose someone you love, I think you understand what you've lost and may never find again." He smiled. "I like to keep you wondering what I'm going to do next."

-"But now it's time I said goodnight. It's freezing cold out here."

They stood there awkwardly regarding one another. Wyatt wanted to kiss her, but waited for Eugenia to give him a signal.

Finally she smiled, "Good night, Wyatt. Someday soon you need to try one of my casserole dishes."

She wanted him to try her casserole! They had made progress. Finally she was starting to come around.

He smiled. "Any time, Eugenia. Any time. I'll see you Saturday at rehearsal."

"See you then." She walked into the house and closed the door, leaving him standing on the porch step, frustrated.

They'd made progress, but he'd really wanted a kiss.

"Damn woman, you had better be worth the trouble."

~

The next day Eugenia glanced around the table at her daughters-in-law and smiled. How different her life was now that her sons were married and had families of their own. This was what she'd wanted when she'd determined to find them wives of their own.

Baby Desirée was showing her spitfire personality, running from room to room, keeping her parents hopping. Sarah and Tanner's son was pulling up, trying to walk. Lucas, Tucker's son, was starting school next year, and his new baby brother or sister was due any day. Three grandkids with another one soon to arrive—life was good.

Yet, she missed having someone to share this with. Wyatt's face swam before her eyes, and she thought it strange she thought of him rather than Thomas.

"Eugenia, are you still with us?"

"Sorry, I was just thinking about how life has changed in the last few years."

The women looked at one another and smiled while they continued to wrap the presents they'd either made or bought for their little ones.

These women she considered her daughters had borne her grandchildren and took care of her sons. She loved them.

"How's the Christmas pageant rehearsal coming?" Rose asked.

"It's going well." Eugenia said, knowing that she was fishing for information about Wyatt.

"Sarah said that Wyatt walked you home last night," Rose said, a twinkle in her eye.

"Yes, he did." Eugenia did not say anything that would confirm the women's interest.

"You know the rumor is that his ranch does very well," Sarah said. "Why, they say he's one of the richest ranchers around here."

"He and Beatrice worked just as hard as me and Thomas to make our spreads successful."

"It's a shame his wife died so young, leaving him alone. He must be lonely living out there in that big house all by himself. I hear his daughter hasn't been home since her mother's funeral," Beth said, her voice soft.

Eugenia glanced around at all the women at the table while inside she was laughing. They were trying to be subtle and not succeeding. "What you're all doing is interfering. I'll make my own decision regarding Wyatt."

Sarah shrugged and gazed at her sisters-in-law and mother-in-law. "What? What are we doing, Eugenia?"

"You're trying to match me with Wyatt, and you're all amateurs." She paused for a moment and chuckled. "Let me just tell you that I am reconsidering my opposition to Wyatt. I'm still undecided and have said nothing to him."

The three women's mouths opened, and then all three started talking at once, excitedly. For a moment, Eugenia sat back and smiled, watching her daughters. These lovely young women were so special. She'd chosen them to marry her sons, and she didn't regret it for one moment.

"What's holding you back?" Rose asked. "I really like him."

"He's so sweet," Beth said.

Eugenia sighed. "Sarah is the only one of you three women who wasn't scrambling to support herself when you met my boys. I'm in a position where I have all the money I need. I can come and go as I please. I don't have anyone depending on me. It's a freeing feeling."

"But don't you get lonely, Eugenia?" Sarah asked. "After I would put Lucas to bed, I felt so alone when I was single. There was no one to talk to about my day or what new thing Lucas was doing."

What Sarah said was true. There was no one to share her joy with about her grandchildren or even her children and what they were doing. Except Wyatt.

"Sometimes. But then I come be with my grandkids. They always cheer me up."

"Your grandkids would still be there if you married Wyatt," Beth said.

They didn't understand. The world was changing for women, and her daughters-in-law were stronger young women than she'd been. And she was glad they stood up to her boys.

"Yes, I know. But I don't have anyone to tell me what I can and can't do. No man to tell me to buy this or I can't serve this, or I didn't do this correctly. Don't get me wrong. I loved Thomas, but he was still a man who let everyone know how he wanted and expected his house to be run. It got old."

"I can understand that," Sarah said. "Sometimes Tucker has pulled that on me, and I just give him a look that tells him that is not territory he wants to enter."

Sarah was the strongest of the three since she'd raised a child without a man's help in the wildest town in the west until Eugenia had brought her home.

"Yes, we all know how Travis can be domineering like his father, but I hope I'm showing him that demanding doesn't always get you what you want," Rose said with a knowing smile.

Eugenia had known Rose was perfect for Travis the moment she saw her stand up to him in the séance parlor she'd once owned.

"Tanner, can be demanding, but it's only going to get him a cold supper, which he hates."

The girls laughed.

Beth's quiet, gentle strength was exactly what Tanner needed. She'd brought her here for Tucker, but Tanner found her first, and she thanked God every day for the mishap that brought her son home.

"I'm so thankful that my sons found and married you girls. I want all of you to be happy."

"And we want your happiness. If that means you want to remain alone the rest of your days, that's your choice," Sarah said.

"Or if you want to marry, Wyatt, that's your choice as well," Rose said.

Eugenia smiled. "Thanks. But to be honest, I don't know what I want." She tied a ribbon around the tissue on the package she was wrapping. "Wyatt is a great man. He's honest and dependable with good morals, he's attractive and friendly. And if I was looking for a husband, I'd look no further. I'm just not certain I want another man to rule my life."

~

On Saturday afternoon, Wyatt glanced outside the church. The clouds were heavy, the air felt damp, and the chill in the air guaranteed only frozen precipitation would fall from the sky. Weather like this didn't happen often in Texas, but when it snowed, everything froze up, and everyone stayed indoors.

He walked over to where Eugenia was working with the three main players of the pageant.

"Eugenia, it's time to end rehearsal. It looks like it's going to start snowing or sleeting any minute," he said, low so as not to alarm the children.

She frowned at him, her blue eyes filled with concern. "I told Scott's mother I'd take him home. Her youngest child was sick, and she didn't want to get her out in the cold."

"Where does he live?"

"A mile from the ranch," she said.

"Then let's leave now," he said, knowing that if snow started to fall, it would soon cover the road, and they could become lost.

"We?"

"I'm not letting you go out in this weather by yourself. I'm going to make certain you get home," he said.

There was no way he would let her drive that buggy home alone in this weather. What if she got stuck? What if the horse became maimed? What if the buggy overturned? No, he was going to drive her home, and then he'd head to his ranch.

"But the children's parents aren't going to pick them up until four. It's only three now."

"Can't Cheryl stay with the children, so we can leave?" he asked, glancing around for the woman, hoping she would agree to stay since she lived in town.

"She didn't come to help today. Her child is sick as well," Eugenia said. "We'll leave once the children have been picked up."

"If it wasn't for Scott, I'd recommend that you stay in town tonight," Wyatt said. He glanced out the window, a nervous tremor racing down his spine.

"I promised his mother, I'd get him home," she whispered.

"Then we need to go soon," he said, walking to the front door where he could watch the changing weather. The temperature had fallen, and he could feel the biting cold seeping in around the door.

"I've got to stay, Wyatt. I have no choice."

He grimaced. "Let's hope the weather holds off."

Fifteen minutes later, a parent walked in. "Mrs. Burnett, I've come to take Timmy home. It's sleeting outside, and I'd recommend that all of you leave now."

Wyatt wanted to leave. He wanted to get going as soon as possible. Weather like this was dangerous.

"Thank you. Once the children are all picked up, we'll leave for home."

Outside, the sky had darkened, and the sleet could be heard hitting the metal roof. The few people out were scurrying along the street, seeking shelter as quickly as possible.

"Okay, kids, I want everyone to clean up and get ready to leave. We're ending rehearsal early today," Eugenia called.

Wyatt paced the floor, watching as one by one the children's parents arrived until only Audelia's daughter, Ruth, remained. Audelia did not walk in until ten after four, and by then the sleet was coming down in torrents.

After the last child was out the door, he turned to Eugenia and Scott. "Are you certain you can't stay in town tonight?"

"No, I promised his mother I would get him home."

"Bundle up. It's cold," Wyatt said as he led them from the church.

Wyatt helped her into the buggy. "Are you sure about going with me to the ranch? Don't you need to get home?"

"My men will take care of the animals. I'm not going to let you drive home in this weather alone. If need to, I'll stay the night at your place."

She frowned but nodded. "Let's go."

Chapter Seven

Wyatt tied his horse to the back of the wagon and crawled into the buggy. "Mind if I drive?"

"Not at all." Relieved was she wouldn't have to drive in this treacherous weather.

"Besides, if we're both in the wagon, we can stay warmer. Or if something should happen, we're together," he said, his eyes never leaving the road.

He pulled the wagon onto Main Street, and the poor horse's hooves slid on the frozen bricks as they gingerly made their way down the deserted street. Every shop, every store, even the saloons had closed early, and only a few people could be seen hurrying along frozen sidewalks, braving the pelting sleet.

At the edge of town, Eugenia considered turning and going back, but once again thought about Scott's mother, who would be worried if the boy didn't get safely home.

Reaching back behind her, Eugenia pulled out a heavy lap blanket. "Wrap this around you. It's going to be a cold ride."

"Yes, ma'am," the kid said, ducking his head against the sleet that rained down on them, making a hissing sound like a snake. "Are we going to make it home?"

"We'll do our best," she told the boy.

An hour later, they pulled into his yard. Even the hounds stayed hidden out of the cold. In the last ten minutes, the sleet had changed to snow and was quickly blanketing the prairie. Once it covered the road, Wyatt would have no idea where the road traveled.

The poor horse shivered and snorted as he stood in front of the house and Scott climbed down out of the buggy. "Be careful, Mrs. Burnett, Mr. Jones."

"We will, Scott," she said, reassuring the boy. For once she felt grateful for Wyatt's presence. This weather frightened her. Her gloves were coated in ice, leaving her fingers numb, and her feet were cold.

"You want to continue on?" Wyatt asked.

Did they have a choice?

"We're not far from the ranch. Let's hurry before the road is covered. You're going to have to spend the night, Wyatt," she said, thinking of her home and Travis and Rose.

"Yes, I think so," he said. "Let's go."

He slapped the icy reins on the back of the horse, and the buggy pulled out of the drive onto the road. The horse plodded along the road as snowflakes fell from the sky faster and faster until Eugenia could barely see ahead of her.

They should have left sooner, or she should have stayed in town. But this kind of snowstorm was rare in Texas, and she thought there would be no problem getting home.

"I haven't seen snow like this in years." Somehow she felt safer with Wyatt sitting beside her.

"This one will go down in the records," he said, his face tense as he stared at the partially covered road.

She gazed across the prairie at the oaks and the mesquite trees covered in white. The area looked surreal with the ground covered as if with a pristine coat of white paint. The last embers of daylight were fading, and she knew that in the next twenty minutes, it would be dark.

"At this pace, we're still at least an hour from the ranch," she said, worry beginning to gnaw at her.

The horse stumbled. "That's too far. It'll be dark soon."

The cold had seeped into her bones, and she felt chilled, her fingers and toes numb. This was dangerous. If the horse snapped a leg, they would be in trouble. Snow covered the road, and in the darkness, how would Wyatt know where to drive the wagon?

"There's a line shack on the edge of our property. I haven't been to it in many years, but it sat off the main road at least a hundred yards. We should be coming up on it anytime," she said, gazing out at the countryside and trying to see the shack.

"We need to stop there. The road is just about covered, and the light is almost gone. I don't know where I'll be driving. We could end up in a ditch," he said, his voice tense unlike she'd ever heard him before. He was rigid sitting on the seat, his gaze on the road.

A prickle of alarm skittered down her spine at the thought of spending the night in the line shack alone with Wyatt. But a howling whirl of snow stung her face, and she knew they had to get out of the elements or die.

No words were exchanged as she scoured the countryside looking for the building that would save their lives. She didn't know how they could continue on without getting lost, and there was no way to return to Fort Worth, as their tracks were now covered by snow.

She'd give everything she had right now for a warm bed, a cup of coffee, and a bowl of soup. Funny how when things became so desperate, what was important became apparent. Wyatt was important. She could never have completed this trip alone.

"There!" Wyatt said. "Off to the left, sitting down from that hill, right there," he said, relief in his voice.

"Yes, that's it," Eugenia confirmed. "And there's a lean-to for the horses."

"Now where is the road leading to that shack," Wyatt said, looking at the ground and searching for telltale signs of a road covered in snow. "I think this is it, but hang on. I could be wrong."

The wagon slid when he turned the corner. Eugenia grabbed his arm, certain they were going to tumble out of the off the seat and into the snow. But it soon straightened up, and the horse kept plodding along, almost as if it sensed they were heading to shelter.

"Thank God, we found it," she said.

"Yes ma'am."

It took another fifteen minutes to reach the building. Wyatt pulled the wagon to a halt in front of the shack, and apprehension filled Eugenia. The building was old faded lumber put together in a square with a tin roof to keep out the weather. There was nothing fancy about the shack other than the fact that it had a stove where they could dry out, get warm, and be out of the weather.

Wyatt jumped down and turned to lift her from the wagon and set her down in the soft snow. The wind whipped and pulled at her bonnet while snow stung her cheeks.

"Let me go in first in case there are any critters nesting inside."

"After you," she said, huddling behind him.

There was no telling what they might find in that building. There was no telling who had been the last person to sleep there. There was no telling what varmint had made this shack its home.

Wyatt opened the door of the shelter and stepped into the dark musty cabin. He pushed aside a cobweb strung across the opening. Inside the door, hanging from a peg, was a lantern. He took it down and pulled a match from the matchbox he found sitting on a shelf. Soon light flooded the small cabin.

"It looks okay," he said, glancing around.

"At least we're out of the weather." She stood next to him gazing at the starkness of their shelter yet grateful to be out of the storm.

They glanced around the one-room shack to the single bed sitting along a wall. A small table and some dishes on a shelf completed the interior. A wood stove stood in a corner, and Wyatt crossed to the contraption. He opened the door and looked inside. A crate of split logs and kindling sat next to the stove.

"Stand back, Eugenia. You never know if the birds or the wasps may have made the stove pipe their home."

Eugenia smiled and rubbed her hands up and down her arms, trying to get them warm. "I'm just so happy to see a lighted stove."

"You and me both," he said. "I was getting worried."

"Me too. I didn't know how we were going to find our way home," she said, her voice shaking from cold and fear and nerves. They were stranded all alone in a cabin with a single bed and enough desire between them to start a fire.

He glanced at her. "But we're okay. We found this shelter, and we can stay here until the storm blows over."

She nodded, too cold to say anything else.

In a matter of minutes, Wyatt had a nice roaring fire started.

He stood up and glanced around the cabin, his eyes finally resting on Eugenia. "Will you be all right while I go out and tend to the horses? I want to get them out of this wind."

"I'll be fine. I'll look around to see if I can find us any food," she said, grateful for a moment alone.

Wyatt walked out the door, his boots making a hollow sound on the floor. She stood there staring at that one bed. She glanced around the room, noting the spare furnishings, the table and chairs, and still her eyes returned to that bed.

A shiver of warm anticipation roared through her body, causing her breathing to quicken. That bed. That blasted, single, tiny bed had her heart racing inside her chest. She couldn't sleep with him.

She peered out the window and saw Wyatt lead the poor horses to the lean-to. It wasn't much, but at least they were out of the wind and snow.

She watched him unbuckle the halter from the horse and settle him down with what looked like hay that must have been left behind.

He'd be back here any minute, and all she'd done was stood in the middle of the room and stare at the bed. That bed that would hold two people. She swallowed and willed her feet to move.

Taking her bonnet off, she shook the snow from the top but left her coat on until the stove warmed up the room. Then she began to look in cupboards for anything to eat. Anything that someone might have left behind.

Travis had the line shacks regularly stocked just in case of a situation like this, so hopefully no one had cleared out the canned food.

She came across some dried beans, rice, peaches, and spiced apples she'd canned last summer.

When she opened up the last cabinet to pull out a pan, a mouse came scampering out the door, and she screamed as he ran around her full skirts and under the bed.

The door to the cabin flew open, and Wyatt came running in. "What's wrong?"

She laughed. "I disturbed a mouse. He frightened me when I opened the cabinet door. He was hiding among the pans."

Wyatt started laughing. "Where did he go?"

"Under the bed," she said, pointing to the spot where the critter had disappeared.

"Do you want me to find him and kill him?" Wyatt asked.

She shook her head and gave a shiver. "If you can find him, but they're pretty quick."

Wyatt lifted the bed, frame and all. The mouse darted out and hid behind the chair. Wyatt dropped the bed and ran over to the chair, where the mouse scooted behind the box of wood. Wyatt ran over to the box of wood, and the mouse disappeared behind a hole in the cabinets.

She couldn't contain her laughter as she stood there watching the big cowboy chase a tiny mouse around the room, his boots making enough noise to send the mouse racing from spot to spot. "I think he's a little faster than you."

Wyatt stopped for a moment, his breathing labored, and smiled. "He must be younger than me."

"If you feel more comfortable with him gone, then the mouse has to go," Wyatt said. His cinnamon brown eyes warmed her from the inside out.

When he looked at her that way, with his gaze all heated and sultry, she wanted to pull him to her and lay her mouth over his until they were both satisfied. But that wouldn't be good. Not now. Not when they were all alone in this tiny cabin with a single bed.

She shook her head and then showed him her finds. "Don't worry about him. You've scared him, and maybe he won't come out again."

He smiled at her. "Good. I would have had a better chance shooting him," he replied. "Did you find any food?"

"We have about two days' worth of food. If you like beans, rice, and fruit."

They wouldn't be here two days. At first light, they would leave for the ranch.

"It's enough to sustain us. Usually this type of a storm blows over in a day. We should be able to leave tomorrow," Wyatt assured her.

"I hope so. My family will be worried," Eugenia said suddenly feeling wistful for her family.

"Yes, Gus will be wondering what's happened to me," he said, his voice trailing off as he turned and stared at the bed.

She couldn't talk about that bed. Not yet. Not with this big man filling up the space in the cabin, making her feel safe, secure, and warm. Not with them all alone for the first time. Her lungs didn't seem to want to work when she thought of the two of them isolated here, all night, with one bed.

She couldn't think about this now. She wasn't ready to face that single bed. "If you'll fill the bucket with snow, I could make us a cup of coffee if you'd like."

"I'd enjoy a cup of coffee, and then I'd like to sit around the fire for a bit and warm up," he said as he went back out into the snow.

"I'll get started on the coffee," she said, needing to do something to keep from staring at that bed.

When he came back in, she packed snow in the coffee pot and put it on the stove.

Wyatt checked the lantern. "We have enough oil to last the night. I think we're good."

He pulled up two chairs close to the stove. "Sit down with me, Eugenia."

Her heart began to pound, and yet she couldn't deny herself sitting next to Wyatt and relaxing for the first time since they'd left the church. She handed him a cup of coffee, and they sat by the fire, sipping from their tin cups and listening to the wind howl outside the cabin, rattling the window panes and sending a shiver down Eugenia's spine.

"Do we have enough wood?" she asked, knowing the cabin would cool off in a hurry when the fire died. "Yes, I found a stack in the lean to, and we've got enough to last us through tomorrow. I'm hoping we'll wake up in the morning and this will be gone," he said, sipping his coffee.

"We don't get much snow, so it shouldn't last long," she said, assuring herself that this was just for tonight. In the morning, he would take her home to the ranch, and they would talk about their adventure. But first they had to get through tonight.

They both stared at the fire.

"I don't need the bed," he said. "You take the bed, and I'll sleep on the floor."

She glanced over at him, and he refused to meet her gaze. "And use what for a pillow and blankets? Do you think there are extra in this cabin?"

He laughed, his brown eyes glinting in the lantern light. "I guess not. But I can bed down on my coat and use your coat as a blanket."

She thought for a moment and considered that might work. She slipped out of her coat, realizing the cabin had finally warmed enough that she could take off the outer layer. She'd sleep in her clothes just to stay warm.

"Did you and Beatrice ever get caught in a situation like this?" she asked, trying to fill the uneasy silence, biting her bottom lip.

He glanced over at her and grinned, his full lips inviting. "No. We outran a tornado once, but it lifted back into the heavens before it got too close to us. Scared us plenty. Margie was just a baby, and I didn't know how I was going to protect them."

His words chased the chill from her bones. She liked the way he was concerned about protecting his family. It reinforced the fact that he was a good man who safeguarded those he loved.

"Were you and Beatrice happy?" she asked. The atmosphere in the cabin was toasty and cozy and unnerving. All she wanted to do was cuddle with him, and that couldn't be good. Maybe talking about their previous spouses would cool the charged atmosphere.

She couldn't let him touch her. She couldn't let him near her.

He raised one brow at her. "I think so. We didn't argue much. I would have liked to have had more children, but her health wasn't good even then. I miss her, but she's gone, and my life goes on. What about you and Thomas?"

She stared at him and contemplated how she could tell him the truth about her marriage. "You could say we were. I loved him, bore him three sons, and we built a good life together."

"Why do I sense that there's a 'but' in there somewhere. You said in the wagon you hated being married. Why?"

She smiled. "Oh yeah, I kind of forgot that I said that to you."

"Well now is a good time to explain that remark."

"Thomas was too controlling. Sometimes he felt like he was more my father than my husband. Don't get me wrong. I loved Thomas. It's just that since he's been gone, I've felt like a free woman. I live my life without anyone saying what I can and can't do. I like it that way. There's no man controlling me."

Wyatt leaned back in his chair and nodded his head, but then he turned those sultry honey-brown eyes on her, and the charm just seemed to ooze from his gaze. So much that she felt flushed just looking at him.

"You're a strong woman, Eugenia. I find it hard to believe that you let your husband control you," he said softly.

Eugenia sighed. Now, she was a strong woman. But she had let Thomas control her. "We married when I was fifteen. I was a kid. I didn't learn to stand up to Thomas until I was in my thirties, and by that time the mold of our marriage had already been cast. He was in control. There were times I put my foot down, and he learned when I said no, it was no, but that took some years."

"But don't you miss the companionship of marriage?"

"No." She knew she lied.

He hung his head for a moment. "I miss Beatrice. I miss the Beatrice that was healthy and vibrant. The woman who cuddled with me, adored me, and made my life better. Not the sick woman who struggled for so many years. That was hard."

"She often told me she hated being ill," Eugenia said.

"I know she did."

Eugenia bit her lip. How could she be jealous of a dead woman? How could she envy what she'd never had? "I never realized how close you and Beatrice were."

"We were very close until she became so ill. Then she shut me out. I think she wanted to prepare me for the worst. While I understand why she did it, I still miss her," he said, not looking at Eugenia but staring into the flames of the crackling stove.

He turned and gazed at Eugenia, his face solemn, his eyes warm. "What if you were married to a man who didn't want to control you? Would you feel differently about marriage?"

She sat back, stunned, her heart pounding, her body tense. She'd never even considered marriage a second time. It hadn't been an option she wanted in her life again.

"I don't know. I like my life now. I'm in control."

"But you're alone," he said. "Beatrice and I were a team. We made decisions together. Neither one of us told the other one what they could and couldn't do. We respected one another enough that we consulted each other and made decisions together. But if she wanted to go do something, I would have had to lock the woman up to stop her. It wasn't my place to control her," he said, his eyes never wavering from Eugenia.

The wind blew hard enough it rattled the door, startling her. She jumped at the noise.

After the shock of losing Thomas had worn off, the years since he'd died were good ones. Years where she'd grown and become more independent than she'd ever dreamed possible for a woman. Being married again sounded like going back to the life where she'd had so little control. She'd never allow another man to dominate her again.

"I don't know a man who doesn't expect his wife to let him lead."

"I don't want a wife who wants to lead. I want a partner."

Her mind reeled from his statement, and yet part of her didn't believe him. She couldn't fathom a marriage where she would be a partner.

Sleet slammed against the window panes, and Eugenia shivered and gave a little shudder. A rumble of thunder rattled the building.

Wyatt looked out the window. "Wow, that's quite a storm. It's a good thing we got out of it when we did."

"Yes, Eugenia said. "Are you hungry?"

His dark eyes turned on her, and his gaze caused a little catch in her throat. Outside the storm raged, and inside there was another storm brewing. A storm that was much more dangerous than the weather. This one involved hearts and bodies and feelings long denied.

Unable to sit still a moment longer, she jumped up, needing to do something. "I'll start up that rice and beans I found."

Her hands were shaking as she found a pan, wiped it out, and then filled it with rice and beans. "It's not going to be too tasty without a little salt pork, but it'll be good enough to stop the hunger pains."

She turned around from the counter, and there was Wyatt right behind her. She ran into his hard chest. She glanced into his brown eyes and saw the fire burning in his gaze. She wanted to lean into his body and give herself over to his kiss, but she feared once his lips touched hers she'd go up in flames. She'd be lost, and that bed, that beacon from the other side of the room, would receive a workout like it'd never had before.

"Uh…" She grabbed the pan from the sink. "I need to get this on the fire. It will take at least an hour if not longer, and it's already late."

"Forget the damn food, Eugenia. The only thing I'm hungry for is you."

"Wyatt…we can't."

She took a deep breath, the center of her body throbbing and pulsing and wanting to give in to Wyatt. Fear sent her scurrying past him, and she placed the beans on the stove.

"We've got to eat, Wyatt. Who knows how long we're going to be stuck in this cabin? It's snowing and sleeting and thundering and…"

A big flash of lightning filled the cabin, and thunder rattled the windows.

She squealed and ran toward him. He opened his arms and wrapped them around her. His embrace was safe and strong and secure, and what the hell was she doing? "That was close."

Wyatt glanced out the window, his arms still tightly wrapped around her. "That one was too close. I was afraid it would have spooked the horses, and then we'd be walking once this all cleared."

"They're still there?" she asked, looking at him and thinking she couldn't do more than one night in this small space with this man. She couldn't do another night of the two of them confined together while her mind created images of the two of them together in that bed, naked.

His gaze met hers and then moved to her lips. "Yes, they're still there."

She slipped out of his embrace, needing to put as much distance as she could between them. If he kissed her, she'd be lost. She'd be in his arms. He'd be in her bed. "I need to check the beans."

Hurriedly she put space between them. She took a deep breath and glanced around the cabin, needing to do something to keep the images in her mind at bay and Wyatt at arm's length.

He walked up behind her and put his arms around her. "You're shaking worse than a bride on her wedding day."

Oh, that was not the image she needed. At least, he hadn't said wedding night.

"I'm cold," she said and didn't move from his arms.

"Yeah, the fire is dying out some. I was trying to save that last log for in the morning. It's going to get cold tonight."

She pulled away from him and stepped to the side of the room. She glanced at the bed and then at Wyatt. "I can't share that bed with you, Wyatt. I'll sleep on the floor."

"There's no way that I'm going to let you sleep on the floor. You can just get that idea right out of your head. I'll be okay."

They stood there staring at one another, an awkward silence filling the cabin. She didn't know what to do.

She sank down into the chair near the fire and gazed into the flames. What were her boys thinking right now? Were they worried about her? Tucker would think she was at the ranch, and Travis would think she was with Tucker, and Tanner would just think she was okay.

Instead, she felt more danger inside this cabin than she'd felt out in the weather. Danger to her heart, not to her health.

He sank down into the chair across from her. "It's getting late. It's going to be a long night, so why don't we go to bed? That way we'll save lantern fuel, and you'll be warmer in bed."

"Okay," she said, licking her lips nervously.

She got up, put a lid on the beans that were just about done, and put them on the counter. They would stay cool enough to last through the night. Right now she couldn't eat a bite. She wasn't hungry for food, but for Wyatt.

Eugenia took a sip of water and realized she'd have to go outside one last time. She turned to glance at Wyatt. She wasn't going to say anything. She would just put her coat on, take the slop jar and go outside. Even in rough weather there were some things a lady didn't share.

Picking up her coat, she shrugged into it.

He stared at her in confusion. "What are you doing?"

She didn't answer but picked up the slop jar. "Oh for Christ sake, Eugenia, you are not going out in that weather."

"Are you telling me what I can and can't do?" she asked, an incredulous look on her face.

"I...oh hell. I need to go check on the horses one last time. Let me go outside, and you can do your business while I'm gone."

"Thanks," she said, grateful not to have to go out in the snow. The storm had slowed some, but icy flakes still fell from the sky.

He shrugged on his coat. "I'll be back in five minutes."

While he was gone, Eugenia hurriedly did her business and then opened the door to empty the jar. The wind blew the door open the rest of the way, and she could see Wyatt down in the lean-to caring for the horses, making certain they were okay.

Snow pelted her face, and she hurriedly shut the door, shivering from the cold. The little shack felt cold again, so she threw the last log on the fire.

She pulled back the blanket on the bed and checked the sheets to make certain no creature had nested up under the coverlet during the summer, and then sank down on the lumpy mattress and took her boots off.

Her feet were still cold. She pulled her petticoat off, but left the rest of her clothes on and crawled beneath the covers. It felt good to lie down. She lay there with her eyes closed, hoping she could pretend she was asleep.

The door blew open, and Wyatt walked in with an armload of wood. "Thought since I was out there, I might as well bring in more wood."

She opened her eyes and looked at him. His hat and his clothes were dusted with snow. God, the man looked like sin wrapped in a nice package.

Her body hummed in appreciation of the man as she watched him, his earthy brown eyes staring at her in the bed. An awkward silence filled the cabin.

He dropped the wood into the log holder and two mice went scurrying across the floor to the cabinets.

"Damn. More mice," he said.

And she was going to make him sleep on the floor. She gazed at the hard wooden planks, and then she stared at this big, strong man.

He shrugged out of his coat and laid it on the floor. He dropped down on his knees, lay down and covered himself with her coat. Just as he reached for the lantern, a mouse scurried across the floor.

"Balderdash! You can't sleep on that floor. When you turn out the lantern, the mice are going to come out to play."

He sighed. "I think you're right."

She scooted to the very edge of the bed on the opposite side. "Get in bed, Wyatt, before I change my mind."

Chapter Eight

The rattling window panes woke Eugenia, and she realized it was morning. An unfamiliar warmth enveloped her, keeping her toasty. Slowly it sank into her brain that an arm circled around her with her back against a very male chest. Something long and hard poked her in the back.

Wyatt. Oh my! It'd been many a year since she'd awoken to the feel of a man snug against her backside and the scent of him surrounding her.

Delicious tingles spiraled through her, awakening her body, reminding her of how long it'd been since she was with a man.

How could Wyatt evoke so many conflicting emotions? Her body betrayed her while her mind doubted her convictions. More and more her heart longed to join with his.

Sometime during the night they must have become entangled, and this morning his warmth cocooned her from the harsh cold in the cabin. She could see her breath frosting the air above their bed. The fire was nothing but charcoals, yet she'd slept better than she could remember.

"Good morning," Wyatt said, his voice a whisper against her hair, her nerves dancing along her spine straight into her groin.

"You were supposed to stay on your side of the bed," she admonished.

"I am. You're on my side," he said with a chuckle.

She glanced at the bed. "Oh."

Her skirt was hiked up near her waist, the material trapping her. Not that she really wanted to move. It felt wonderful to be lying here like this with Wyatt. It was warm, sensual, and her body was pulsing in ways she'd long since forgotten. Waking up sheltered in his arms, there couldn't have been a better way to start the day.

"I guess we should get up." she said, not really desiring to move.

"Why?" he asked. "It's cold outside these covers. I can see it's still snowing, and frankly, I like you lying here next to me," he said, his voice deep and low in her ear, sending tremors down her spine.

"It's wrong, Wyatt," she whispered.

"Nothing wrong with two people who care about each other keeping one another warm."

Well, when he put it that way, it was true. She did care about Wyatt, more than she thought possible. She just didn't wish to marry him. "I'd forgotten what waking up with a man feels like."

"I'd forgotten what waking up with a woman feels like," he said, his voice even deeper, sending delicious shivers of need through her. "I'm sure there are other things we've forgotten, too."

An image of the two of them making love filled her mind. It wasn't Thomas anymore that permeated her thoughts, it was Wyatt. And God forgive her, she wanted him. Wanted him like she'd never wanted before. Wanted him like she couldn't survive without touching him.

Suddenly she rolled over and faced him, still curled in his embrace, and lifted her face to gaze into those earthy brown eyes and felt her lungs seize. "Wyatt..."

"Yes, Eugenia," he said, his mouth inches from hers, as if he was holding back from kissing her.

"It's been a long time since I've been in bed with a man," she said, only knowing that she needed this man, and she had to have him now.

"I've haven't been in bed with a woman since before Beatrice passed."

She placed her hand on his chest, running it up over his shoulder. "I know some would consider what I'm going to say is wrong. But we're here, in this bed..." she licked her lips and gazed into his eyes, needing him to understand but yearning for him just the same. "I still don't want to get married. But could we…for just today, for just this moment act like we're married?"

"Oh Gawd, woman. I thought I was going to have to go outside in the snow to take care of…" His lips came down on hers, and this time his kiss was demanding, not gentle or caressing. This time his mouth possessed hers, and she welcomed that possession. She needed this man right now.

His lips covered hers, and the doubts she'd held were banished as his tongue caressed the inside of her mouth, swirling and building a need she'd long since forgotten. He rolled her over onto her back, his lips never leaving hers as he kissed her until she thought she'd faint from the mounting pleasure.

She put her hand to his chest to push him away. "Wyatt, I'm not a young woman any longer. My body's not…"

"I don't care. I want you," he said, his lips covering hers again, leaving her dizzy, her body more alive than she could remember.

He pulled back and stared into her eyes. "Are you certain about this?"

Her stomach clenched at the thought of him stopping. She reached up and began to unbutton his shirt. "Shut up, Wyatt, and get rid of these clothes."

He laughed and rolled off her and began to remove his clothes under the blankets. When he finished unbuttoning his shirt, she pulled it off his back and tossed it to the floor. Next came his pants, and once they were unbuttoned, she pushed his trousers down, until he kicked them off along with his long underwear and threw them to the floor.

Naked, he rolled towards her. "Now it's your turn," he said and rolled her to her side to unbutton her dress.

Eugenia could feel his nimble fingers as he undid the buttons. He placed his lips along her back, and she shivered from the feel of his mouth against her spine.

"Hurry, Wyatt," she said softly.

"Patience, woman," he replied, kissing the back of her neck.

She'd never experienced being with a man like this before. She'd never ached so badly for a man that she threw all caution to the wind and only coveted the feel of his naked skin caressing hers. She'd never guarded her heart and yet given him her body.

With a gasp she quickly helped him shed her dress. A pull of the bow untied her chemise and lifted the garment over her head. And then she untied her bloomers and kicked them off.

She lay beneath the covers completely naked. He trailed his fingers from her shoulder past her hip. Gently he turned her over, and she faced him.

"God, Eugenia, you've never been more beautiful than you are right now."

Their gazes locked, and in a not too subtle exchange as he expressed the need she knew her own eyes reflected.

She reached up and pulled him down to her, needing his lips to cover hers once more and vanquish her doubts. She craved him more than her next breath, but she didn't need to marry the man. She only desired this moment of pleasure.

His lips released hers, and he kissed her neck, her chest until his mouth reached her breast, and he covered her nipple. She moaned as his tongue laved her hardened nipple, his teeth gently nipping her as he suckled her breast, sending tingles all the way to her middle.

So many years had passed since she'd felt loved. Never had she been so wanton, and yet it felt good.

She ran her hands along his back, feeling the strong muscles that girded this man. As she traced his ribs with her fingertips, he shivered in her arms, and she kissed the top of his head. Emboldened, she reached down and touched his throbbing member. He jumped when she wrapped her fingers around that solid muscle and caressed him.

"Oh, Eugenia, you know how to torture a man," he said against her breast.

His tongue ravished her breasts, building a delicious sense of heat and need between her legs. Lost in the sensations his touch evoked, she moved her hips in an urgent invitation.

Sensing her unrest, his hand cupped her feminine mound and she moaned. "Oh yes, Wyatt."

His fingers parted her folds and delved inside her. She gasped with pleasure as he stroked her until she thought she would faint from need. He stroked her until she was about to beg him for release. He stroked her until she was gasping with pleasure, her body needing the release only he could give.

He removed his lips from her breasts and moved his body in between her legs. "Eugenia, I wish this could last forever, but I'm near the edge."

"Wyatt, just love me to completion," she whispered, needing him inside her now.

In one swift movement, he thrust inside her, filling her to the hilt. She gasped at the pleasure and wrapped her arms around him, moaning into his strong shoulder.

With each touch, she craved more of this man and with each kiss she experienced more pleasure than she'd dreamed possible. With each stroke, she surrendered more to Wyatt.

Desire reflected from his brown eyes, and she felt like she was looking into his soul. Intimacy she'd never experienced before shown in his gaze as he stared at her, so loving and sweet that she didn't want to leave this place. She didn't want to end these minutes in his arms.

A tightening spiral of pleasure so intense she couldn't remember experiencing anything like it before wound through her until she thought she would die and cross to the other side.

Shattering contractions and releases shook her just as Wyatt cried out her name.

"Eugenia," he said and plunged into her one last time, rocking her with him and shuddering his release.

The wind howled outside while they lay there holding one another, their bodies recovering, her heart aching and almost bursting with feelings she didn't want to acknowledge.

She'd never experienced such powerful, emotional sex. Never. What did she do now?

Wyatt kissed her gently, rolled off of her and pulled her into his chest, spooning her. He pulled the covers up, tucking them under their chins to keep their naked bodies warm.

"Woman, you may not like hearing it, but we belong together. I told you we'd burn up the sheets, and by God, it's a wonder this cabin didn't catch fire," he said into her ear, his voice soft.

"Don't ruin it. No talk of marriage this day. Let's just enjoy our time together and tomorrow we'll talk about the consequences of today."

～

Thirty minutes later, Wyatt had dressed and stepped outside to give Eugenia time to clean up and dress alone.

Though she wasn't shy, it was nice to have the cabin to herself for a moment or two. And it gave her time to pull herself back together. Time to tame the wild beating of her heart and harden the way she regarded Wyatt. She couldn't let this tender moment soften the way she thought with regards to marriage.

Tying her shoe laces, she glanced over at the bed and sighed. What had she done? She'd slept with a man that she wasn't married to, but yet it had felt right. So right that it frightened her. She was not going to remarry. Never.

She quickly made the bed, choosing not to see the indentations of their bodies any longer. She stoked the fire that Wyatt had started and filled the coffeepot. Wyatt would come in cold and hungry.

A quick glance out the window saw the man giving the horses fresh water and hay. Thank God there had been a supply of food for the animals and even a stack of firewood.

The sky was beginning to lighten, but snow still sprinkled like a light shower from the clouds. The accumulation was probably three inches, and she was sure her grandson would soon be out in the stuff making a snowman.

She watched Wyatt walking toward the cabin, his arms loaded with more wood. She ran to the door to open it for him.

"Thanks, Eugenia," he said, stomping his feet before he entered the tiny cabin. He dumped the wood in the wood box.

"How are the horses?"

"Good. I'll go out later and walk them around the yard. It's not good for them to be standing there that long."

"I'll go with you," she said, thinking they had to get out of this cabin or they'd find themselves back in bed.

He nodded. "Might be good to get outside for a while. The roads are still covered, and snow is still falling. I don't believe we should try to leave today. What do you think?"

She smiled. She wasn't ready for this to end. She wasn't ready for them to be with people again. She wanted this time alone with Wyatt because when it was over, it was over.

"Let's just spend today at the cabin and then we can head on to the ranch tomorrow," she said, imagining another night in Wyatt's embrace. One more night before it was over.

"You sit down and I'll fix us both a cup of coffee. We can sit near the stove and warm up," he said, moving towards the counter.

For a moment, she looked at him, startled. Thomas had never brought her a cup of coffee the entire time they were married.

She watched Wyatt pour coffee into the cup and then hand it to her. He picked up the pan of beans and put them on the stove to heat. Then he joined her by the fire. "I worked up quite an appetite this morning."

His remark had her cheeks burning, but she couldn't help but smile. They'd been good together. Too good.

He leaned over and kissed her on the lips. "Damn, woman, you made me a happy man today."

Her stomach tightened and spread warmth through her body. "Shut up, Wyatt. You're just sweet-talking me."

"It's true."

They sat in silence, sipping their coffee. She had never been so relaxed, as if she was floating in the room with this wonderful man. Had she ever felt this way before?

"I don't want to dwell on our past spouses, but I need to know something." Eugenia said, staring at her coffee cup, unable to meet his gaze. "Was it—this morning—was it always like that with you and Beatrice?"

Wyatt laughed. "No. Not really. Not even when we were first married. Bernice was a good woman, but she didn't like being with me. Hell she probably wouldn't have liked it with any man." He gazed at her, his earthy brown eyes questioning. "What about you and Thomas?"

Eugenia sighed and took a sip of her coffee. "It was good. I remember enjoying being with him. Lovemaking was easy, but being his wife was not. But I have to say, Wyatt, that..." She glanced over at the bed. "It was breathtaking."

He grinned. "Thank you, ma'am, glad I could please."

She hit his arm with her arm, and yet she couldn't stop smiling. She felt good. She felt wonderful, and she felt more alive at this moment than she had in years. "You're quite pleased with yourself."

He picked up her hand and brought it to his lips. "I want to make you happy. I want to be the man who makes you smile. I want you to look forward to seeing me each day. I want to go to bed at night and hold you in my arms. I want to come home each day hungry for your welcoming smile. I want you to ma—"

Panic seized her middle.

"Stop! Don't say what I think you're about to say." Her chest tightened as if it would explode, her mind swirling with so many questions. How could she turn away this man who was so earnest, so kind? She squeezed his hand. "Please, Wyatt, let's just enjoy this day together. Tomorrow we can have a serious talk."

Wyatt stood and circled the small cabin. His jaw was tight and tense, and his eyes clearly reflected his frustration. She stood and walked up behind him and slipped her arms around him. "I'm afraid, Wyatt. Please, let's just enjoy today."

He turned in her arms and held her. "Okay. But tomorrow morning before we leave, we're having a serious conversation about us."

She nodded, knowing that whatever she said tomorrow would either end or begin this relationship. But she needed time to think. Her heart would like to claim him, but her head kept reminding her of the chains of marriage.

"Agreed."

"The beans are boiling. Let's eat, and then we could play checkers," she offered.

"Can we do it naked?" he asked, his expression sincere, his brows raised in a questioning way.

She laughed. "No, at our age that's not always a pretty sight. But we can play to see who is in charge the next time we go to bed?"

Yes, she wanted him again. As long as they were in this cabin, she wanted Wyatt. She'd enjoy him just as long as she could.

He grinned, his eyes twinkling with happiness. "So we're going to do it again?"

She smiled and shook her head at his delight. "What else are we going to do?"

Wyatt looked up at the ceiling. "Lord, thank you for this storm, and could you keep it up for a week?"

"We'd starve."

He shrugged. "Who needs food when I have you here all to myself," he said, his low voice sending a delicious shiver through her body. When would she stop desiring him? When would she get enough?

"So you're no longer hungry?" she asked.

"I'm starving for you again, just as soon as we eat breakfast. At my age, a man needs to protect his strength," he said, rubbing his belly.

She laughed and couldn't remember a recent morning filled with such joy. "I'll get us some bowls."

~

After breakfast, they decided to go out and walk the horses. The clouds were no longer a deep, dark blue, but had lightened to a grey, and now only an occasional snow flake fell. Tomorrow morning the sun would probably be shining, and the storm would be over. So would her time with Wyatt.

Bundled in her coat, with her mittens on and her scarf wrapped tightly around her, they ventured out into the snow. The first step out of the cabin, she sank into the snow all the way to the top of her boots. Wyatt held her arm as they staggered toward the wooden lean-to, her skirt dragging in the snow.

"I don't think I'll slip and fall," she told him. "But my dress is getting wet."

"I know, but I kind of like holding on to you," he said, smiling at her, his brown eyes filling her with warmth. "And your dress we can hang by the fire to dry."

She laughed at him, yet a ripple of awareness went through her at the idea of going without her dress. "You're naughty."

"No, I just like to look at you."

When they reached the lean-to, he let go of her arm and went inside. He slipped the bridle onto her horse and led the mare out into the snowy yard. The horse snorted and sauntered along with Wyatt talking to her softly.

Eugenia walked alongside Wyatt and the mare while she gazed out at the frozen countryside. Everything was dripped in white. The trees, scrub brush, and prairie had ripples of white where the wind had made small drifts. "It's been years since we've had this much snow."

"It's pretty, but I'm glad we don't get it very often," Wyatt said, turning the horse and walking the other direction.

They exercised the mare long enough that Eugenia's toes started to freeze and she began to shiver.

Wyatt put the mare back in the lean-to and retrieved his horse.

"Come on, Sally," he said. "Let's do a little walking."

"Why did you name your horse Sally?"

He shrugged. "I always had a fondness for the name and would have named my daughter Sally, but Beatrice said no."

He turned the mare in the opposite direction and Eugenia followed beside him, enjoying his companionship even if they weren't saying much.

"What about you?" Wyatt asked. "What would you have named your daughter? Eugenia?"

"Dear God, no. My mother saddled me with this name, and I hated it," she said. "I think I would have gone with Corabell or Elizabeth." She pushed through the snow, her skirts dragging alongside Wyatt. "What would your daughter think if you were to marry again?"

She didn't know why that question just seemed to slip out, but also it seemed like important information she needed to know.

He shrugged. "I don't know. I hope she'd be accepting since she lives so far away and I only get to see her once or twice a year. It's not good for a man to live alone."

She gazed at him. "Have you been lonely? You have all those men working for your ranch. You're surrounded by people."

"Yes. I've been lonely for a long time. Even before Beatrice passed on. We were happy, but once she became sick, we didn't have much of a marriage. I've hungered for more. I'm going to have more with someone."

Surprised to hear him admit to being lonely, she failed to see the frozen puddle on the ground. Her foot slid, and she threw her arms up trying to catch herself. Then she was falling.

With a plop, she landed in the snow.

Wyatt dropped the reins of the horse and hurried to her side. "Are you all right?"

She sat up laughing. Her skirt had come up, and she'd landed on her drawers, which were rapidly becoming wet. "I'm fine. A little cold, but fine."

He leaned down, his lips found hers, and he kissed her. Her body softened, and she melted into his kiss as she reached up and shoved a handful of snow on his face.

He gasped.

"Just thought I should bring down your temperature a bit," she said with a laugh, wanting nothing more than to have a good roll in the snow with him.

"It's going to take more than that little bit of snow," he said. "Come on, I'll help you up."

Reaching out his hand, she grasped it, and just as her feet came underneath her, she saw him starting to slide.

"Oh no…" she cried as he fell to the ground and she went down beside him.

She couldn't help but laugh at the sight they made, both of them on their backsides in the snow. Yet she worried he could be hurt. "Are you all right?"

He lay in the snow beside her. "Other than my pride smarting a bit, I think I'm fine."

The horse whinnied.

"You look pretty funny lying there in the snow," Eugenia said. She crawled over to him and checked to make certain he wasn't hurt.

He grinned at her. "You don't look any better. In fact, I see snow in your bonnet."

She sat up. "Should we try this again?"

"Let me go first and I'll pull you up."

He got to his knees, and just as he stood, she watched his boots start to slide.

"Be careful."

Finally he was standing, looking down at her. "You know I think there's some ice beneath us. I'm going to walk around and see if I can pull you up this way."

He moved behind her and pulled her up. "Don't walk over there."

She brushed the snow off of herself, and then she started brushing the powdery white stuff off him. His backside had snow and mud on his pants. Without thinking, she reached up and brushed her hands over his firm butt and down his long, shapely legs.

Even at this age, the man had a body made of steel. A body that she enjoyed. A body that made her heart beat a little faster. A body that she couldn't wait to try again.

Finally she looked at herself. "I'm a mess. I'm frozen, and I can't feel my toes."

"Why don't you go to the cabin and start cleaning up? I'll be there as soon as I put the horse back in the lean-to."

"You don't have to tell me twice."

"Be careful," he said. "I'll be there just as soon as I finish here."

"I'll make a fresh pot of coffee."

"Sounds warm."

Five minutes later when Wyatt walked into the cabin, she had added another log to the fire and put on a pot of water to heat. There was a wooden bathtub sitting in the middle of the tiny room.

"Look what I found outside leaning against the wall of the shack."

He smiled, his brown eyes dancing with delight. "Looks big enough for two."

She could feel her cheeks blush. The idea of the two of them together in that tub had her imaging all kinds of things that had her heart racing. "I hadn't thought of us using it. I was going to wash clothes in it."

"First us and then the clothes," he said, shedding his coat.

Eugenia gazed at him and shook her head, feeling a little nervous about bathing with Wyatt. It seemed so intimate, so personal. "I don't think I've ever bathed with a man before."

"I've certainly never bathed with a woman before. It's a first for both of us," he said.

"But…we were under the covers this morning. It's daylight and well…"

He ambled over and kissed her full on the mouth, his hands bringing her buttocks in close. He whispered against her lips, "I promise not to look. Much."

She swatted him on the arm. "Do you think that makes me feel better?"

"Honey, believe me, we won't be in that tub long. I'm already hard just pondering you and me naked in that warm water."

She laughed, and her breathing quickened at the picture his words conjured up in her mind. "Wyatt!"

Suddenly it dawned on her to wonder how she could ever face this man after this day. How could they go on? "How am I going to look at you without everyone knowing what we've done?"

"If you were my wife, it wouldn't be a problem." He held up his hands. "Just saying, and you brought it up, not me."

He turned his back to her, picked up the kettle and poured it into the tub. Sinking onto the chair, he removed his wet boots and put them next to the fire to dry. "Sit down, and I'll pull off your boots for you."

Remove her boots? Really? The man was waiting on her? She sank onto the chair and he untied her boots and pulled them from her feet. When he removed her wet socks, he laid them by the fire.

"Turn around, and I'll help you with your dress."

"Wyatt?" she said, gazing at him, wondering if he were serious. "Are we really going to take a bath?"

"Why not? It will warm us up. What else are we going to do?" he asked, his expression innocent.

She bit her lip. "I found a bar of soap and even a towel in the cupboard."

"Great," he said, undoing the buttons on her dress. He leaned over and kissed the back of her neck and along her throat. Her knees felt weak, and she leaned back into him, offering him more of her neck.

He tugged off her wet dress and laid it over the chair to steam by the fire. Then he helped her remove her chemise and finally her pantaloons. Awkwardly, she stood there without a stitch of clothes on in broad daylight.

"Wyatt, I've had three babies. I'm almost fifty."

He kissed her mouth, her neck, his hands gripping her face. "I don't care, Eugenia. All that matters is that you're here with me."

His words warmed her, and she realized he made her feel cherished.

He stepped back and started to remove his shirt. "Ladies first. I thought you might like a few minutes in the tub before I join you."

She stared at him in surprise. Why was this man always so thoughtful, so kind? Would marriage be different with this man?

She stepped over the edge of the tub and sank into the warm water. She sighed at the bliss that overcame her. She'd been cold. She'd been achy from the fall, and this was the perfect remedy. She leaned back, and though it wasn't a huge tub, it was long enough she could at least rest her back against the rim.

With a sigh, she half-closed her eyes until she heard him remove his pants, and then she opened them and stared at the proud man standing there nude.

"Ready for some company?" he asked.

"Are you sure we can both fit in here?"

"We'll make room."

He poured more water into the tub, careful not to let the hot liquid touch her skin. Then he climbed in behind and sat her between his knees. It was a tight fit, but when she leaned back against his warm chest, it felt so right.

"Not bad," she said. "I thought you were crazy for wanting us to take a bath, but this feels so nice."

"Told you," he said, his lips close to her ear. His low voice sent ripples of pleasure along her spine.

She could feel his penis hard against her back. "You were right when you said we wouldn't be in here long."

He chuckled. "That obvious?"

"Oh yeah."

"I can't help it, Eugenia. You do this to me. Not Myrtle or any of those other casserole-toting women you were sending me. Just you."

She sighed and pulled his arms around her. For today, this man was hers, all hers, and she was going to enjoy every bit of him. "Would you wash my back? And my front? And any other parts you might find interesting?"

"I thought you'd never ask," he said.

Chapter Nine

Eugenia awoke just like the day before, but this time, she and Wyatt were naked as the day they were born. This time, her back was snug against his chest, her leg entwined with his, skin against skin.

Yesterday after the bath, they had made love once more, and then together the two of them had washed their clothes in the bathtub. The two of them. They had done everything together, and while she wanted to believe that if she married him, life would be like this, a voice of doubt kept telling her he was just being nice.

Once they began to live as man and wife, things would change. He would change. She'd be back to taking care of a man, waiting on him, cooking for him, cleaning for him, only doing what he wanted, and she wasn't ready to give up her freedom for incredible sex.

They had fun together. She enjoyed being with Wyatt. He was everything she'd ever want in a husband if she were looking for a man. But there was no reason for her to marry again.

And then she had the most outrageous, naughty idea. Would Wyatt be agreeable to them slipping off occasionally to this cabin? They could meet and spend the day together, right here in this bed.

His lips nuzzled her neck, and a delightful tremor wound its way from her neck straight to her groin. She sighed. "Good morning, Wyatt."

"Good morning, Eugenia. Hungry?"

"Famished, for you," she said, her body pulsing with need.

He groaned. "You're a hard woman to please."

"And you enjoy pleasing me."

"More than you'll ever know."

His lips kissed a trail down her naked back, and she shivered as his fingers reached around to massage her nipples. She ran her hands along his strong legs and found his manhood hard and ready. She grasped the taught muscle in her hands and squeezed.

He gasped. "Jesus, Eugenia."

She laughed and continued her sweet torture of him as she ran her hands along his shaft, teasing and tempting. His breathing was harsh in her ears, and she loved his reaction to her caresses. Soon he flipped her onto her back and covered her body with his.

Sweet desire filled her as she gazed up into his brown eyes and lost herself in his embrace. In a matter of moments, his fingers found her center, teasing her, torturing her with his caress. She moaned, and her heart filled with an ache that only Wyatt evoked.

As she stroked him, he plunged two fingers into her, and she couldn't remember a time in her life she'd ever felt more loved. A time when lying with a man had her more aroused and needy than her next breath.

She couldn't remember making love ever being this good with Thomas, and she wondered why they'd never had this much fun.

Quickly, Wyatt entered her in one solid thrust, joining their bodies and their souls. She wrapped her legs around him, needing him close, eliciting a groan from him. His lips found hers, and he consumed her, his mouth moving over hers, his hands wringing moans from her as he plunged deep inside her.

Over and over he stroked her while his other hand skimmed her body, caressing her, making her feel like she was a cherished woman that he loved. She'd never felt so special, so loved, so regarded.

Her control slipped as the contractions built within her, and then Wyatt was there, holding her, crying out her name as he took them both over the edge. He held her as the two of them reached the summit and plunged over the side in a grasping almost-death experience.

For a moment they were both silent as they lay there. Her heart hammered in her chest, and her breathing was harsh as she willed her overexcited body to return to normal, slowing her pulse.

Wyatt rolled off of her and pulled her to him, adjusting the blanket so they were both covered. "I love lying here naked with you.

"Hmm, it's nice," she said, still in an afterglow fog that had her gasping for air.

Just then, the door burst open.

Wyatt sat straight up in bed. Eugenia held tight to the covers, her heart pounding in her chest as her three sons stepped through the door.

Oh no! What she'd hoped to keep secret now lay exposed to her children.

Her sons stared at her as if she'd lost her mind. And maybe she had. Reality blew into their make-believe world, shattering the dream quality.

"What the hell?" Travis said, staring at his mother.

"Mom?" Tanner asked.

Tucker just stood there looking at the clothes strung around the cabin to dry, shaking his head, and laughing.

"Boys..." Eugenia squealed, wondering how she would explain this away.

"Wyatt, I think we need to have a little chat about our mother and you," Travis said, walking toward the bed.

Wyatt held up his hands as if he were being arrested. "Now wait a minute. I've been asking your mother to marry me for months, and she's refused, so don't get the wrong idea here. In fact, why don't you boys step outside long enough for us to get dressed, and then we can talk about this situation like civilized folks."

Eugenia knew her sons, and her chest tightened like a cinch on a horse. There would be hell to pay for this incident.

~

As soon as the door closed, Eugenia sprang out of the bed. "Oh poppy-cock, I didn't want them to know."

She pulled her clothes off the line and started to yank them on, her movements sharp and quick.

Wyatt moved to the side of the bed, stood, and leisurely began to pull his pants on. "Honey, it's okay. We'll just assure them that we're going to meet with the preacher just as soon as the roads clear."

Eugenia stopped and stared at him. "Haven't you been listening?"

"Of course I have," he said, bewildered.

"I don't want to get married. No one will force me to marry," she said, jerking on her petticoat.

She pulled her stockings on one by one. When she went to put her dress on, she noticed that Wyatt was sitting, watching her, and not saying a word.

"What?" she asked. "Hurry. The boys are standing outside in the cold."

Wyatt stared at her, his eyes dull as flint, his expression bitter. "Tell me something, Eugenia. Have these two days meant nothing to you? You're still not going to marry me after the time we've spent together?"

She stopped lacing up her shoes and gazed at Wyatt. For a moment, she felt torn. If she were to remarry, Wyatt would be the man she'd go to the judge with. But she didn't want to relinquish her independence.

"These past two days have been wonderful. But I…I don't want to answer to any man."

Wyatt took a deep breath and began to dress again. He wouldn't look at her.

"Do you understand?"

He yanked on his shirt and hurriedly buttoned the front and stuffed it into his pants. "No, Eugenia, I don't think I'll ever understand. Thomas must have made your life hell for you to give up what we shared this weekend."

Fear flooded through her, and she realized she didn't want to lose Wyatt. "Why can't we just remain friends? We could sneak off and meet here once a week."

His body stiffened, and his eyes expanded as he stared at her, fiery fury reflecting from his gaze. The heat was enough to start a roaring inferno. "I refuse to sneak around to be with you. At this point, you either marry me, or we go our separate ways."

She bit her lip and then sighed. "I just can't marry again."

Wyatt walked over and opened the door. "Come on in, boys."

They came in, and Eugenia hurriedly threw the blanket over the bed.

"During the storm, I followed your mother home to make certain she arrived safely. When it got so bad we had to stop, I offered to sleep on the floor, but that didn't happen. We spent the last two nights here, waiting for the snow to melt. I've asked your mother to marry me, but she's said no. So this event stays between us."

Travis glared at Eugenia. "Why the hell won't you marry the man?"

"I have my reasons."

Tanner stepped up and frowned at his mother. "If you'd caught one of us in this position, you'd have insisted that we marry. I think the same should go for you."

Eugenia lifted her chin. "If I'd caught one of you boys with a woman, there could have been the possibility of a baby. There's no chance of a baby for me. I'm your mother, and I said no."

Tucker shook his head and frowned. "They're adults. Leave them be. He's probably better off without her."

"Tucker Burnett," Eugenia said.

He shrugged. "Wyatt's a good man. You're all about matchmaking people to fall in love, but when it happened to you, you choose to run. Seems kind of hypocritical if you ask me."

Her stomach lurched, and she couldn't deny Tucker's accusations. He was right. She enjoyed matchmaking other people, just not herself.

Wyatt grabbed his hat. "Boys, don't disrespect your mother."

He slammed his hat on his head and stared at Eugenia. "I'll see you at the Christmas play."

Tears pricked the back of her eyelids, and her heart filled with pain. He was leaving, and while she understand and knew he had to go, she didn't want him to leave. She didn't want their time together to end this way.

"Good-bye, Wyatt."

He walked out the door, and she sank onto a chair. She knew he would not be back. She had what she wanted, her freedom, and somehow it didn't feel as good as she remembered. Somehow her heart was breaking.

~

The most excruciating silence she'd ever experienced filled the ride to the house. Her boys were angry, and it wasn't Wyatt they blamed, but her.

Although the Texas sun blazed in the sky, a cold wind blew that seeped through Eugenia's clothes, into her pores and lungs, slowing her blood until her heart felt sluggish and frozen. She wanted to cry, but she knew her tears would only freeze on her cheeks.

What had she done?

Travis sat like an unyielding rock beside her, driving the wagon.

"Mom, he's a good man."

"Stay out of it, Travis. This is between me and Wyatt."

"No, you made it about all of us when you slept with him without a ring on your finger," he said, his voice tight with anger.

She turned and stared at her son. "Did you and Rose sleep together before there was a ring on her finger?"

Travis frowned.

"Exactly. You may think I don't know what's going on in my own home, but I do. That old house has a lot squeaks and groans, but there are other times when the noises don't come from the house." Eugenia released a deep breath, frost glittering the air. "I would have said something if I wasn't certain you would eventually marry her. You were meant for Rose."

"You're meant for Wyatt," Travis said, his voice strong and sure.

"I was meant for only one man, your father," she said, although quickly her mind said liar. These last few days had been more fantastic than the entire time she'd been with Thomas. Why? Why did it seem like she was making a mistake?

"Do you think that we're going to be upset that you married again?" Travis asked, giving her a quick glance before he returned his eyes to the road.

"No, but you're a lot like your father. Your father told me when and where and how to do things. He even tried to tell me how I should arrange the kitchen, and I told him to let me please have one part of my world where he wasn't in total control. You need to be careful with how you tell Rose what to do," she said, thinking she'd warned her son about not turning out like his father.

Travis shook his head at her. "You don't get it, do you?"

Eugenia looked at her oldest son, wondering what it was she didn't understand. She'd been married more years than he had. She knew marriage. He hadn't even wanted to get married.

"Yes, I can be damn bossy at times, but my wife lets me know immediately when I cross the boundaries. She's my partner, my helpmate, and she's a damn strong one. Maybe it wasn't Papa that had the problem. Maybe it was you." He paused and gave her a look that left her reeling on the inside. "Maybe you weren't a strong enough partner to stand up to Papa. Maybe you should have set the boundaries of what you were willing to accept and made sure that no one crossed them. You do that now. Why was it different with Papa?"

Eugenia sat back and didn't say a word. Hadn't she been a strong partner for Thomas? Had she let him walk all over her? Had she let him get away with being domineering? Could the problem have been her?

~

When they arrived at the ranch, Rose and Beth came running out of the house, worried expressions on their beautiful faces, and Eugenia felt sick in the pit of her stomach.

"Are you all right?" Rose asked, her green eyes staring at Eugenia.

"We were so worried when you didn't come home," Beth said as she wrung her hands. "I'm so glad they found you."

"I'm fine. The snow was falling so fast and hard we had to stop at the line shack," Eugenia said, climbing down from the wagon. "We couldn't see the road."

"We?" Rose asked.

Eugenia frowned and watched as Travis walked away. "Let's go in the house where it's warm."

They went inside, the three women stomping their feet to remove the snow from their boots. Eugenia went to the kitchen and put the tea kettle on to boil. She needed a cup of the brew to warm her and settle her wayward heart.

She needed something to keep her hands busy, her mind occupied.

She sank down onto the kitchen table and savored the feel of being home, in her kitchen, in the home where she raised the boys, where her grandchildren were growing up, where most of her life had been spent. This was her home.

The women sank onto chairs around the table.

"Where are the boys?" Eugenia asked.

"Uh, they said they needed to tend to some chores," Rose said. "What's going on?"

Eugenia raised her gaze to stare at her daughters-in-law. She sighed, her heart heavy, wishing she could go to her room and hide away. "They're angry at me."

"Travis wasn't happy," Rose said. "What happened?"

Eugenia gave them a quick explanation of what had transpired, leaving out the part about having had the most incredible sex she'd ever experienced. When she finished, they glanced at one another and then at her.

"Why won't you marry him?" Rose asked, her green gaze boring a hole into Eugenia's soul, as if she was trying to understand her reasoning.

"I like my life. I like having control over the decisions I make. It's been peaceful since Thomas died and quit telling me how to live my life. You girls have to remember, I married him at fifteen. I was a girl and went into raising kids and helping with the ranch."

"Do you love Wyatt?" Beth asked.

Eugenia put her hand to her mouth. A little sob escaped, leaving her chest tight with unshed emotions.

There were so many things about Wyatt that she loved. The way he made her laugh, the way he did things with her, the way he treated her, the way he looked after her safety, the tenderness she saw in his eyes.

Was this love? Again? At her age? Was it possible?

Oh God, no, it couldn't be.

She shook her head. "If I were going to get married again, he would be the man I want. But I'm never going to remarry."

The sound of the tea kettle whistle suddenly filled the silent kitchen, causing Eugenia to jump. This was her home, her family, her life. She didn't want more. This was enough.

"Can I ask you girls a question?"

"Sure," Rose said, and Beth nodded.

"When your husband tells you what to do, do you stand up to him?" Eugenia asked, knowing that both women had stood up to her sons, but did they continue to do so, or had they let the men take over since their marriage?

Rose and Beth started laughing.

"What's so funny?" she asked.

"Of course I do. If I didn't, Travis wouldn't have married me. It's what makes our relationship so unique. We each are strong personalities who speak our minds," Rose said, acting as if she was surprised Eugenia would ask.

"Why are you asking?" Beth wanted to know.

"Travis told me that perhaps I wasn't a strong enough person when I was married to his father," Eugenia said, still finding his words deeply troubling.

Beth smiled. "From what Tanner tells me, Thomas Burnett was very opinionated and strong willed. We didn't know you back then, but you're not a weak woman, Eugenia. You defied three sons who didn't want to get married and found them women."

"I always thought I was strong. But now I'm questioning my part in my marriage. Was I too weak?" she asked, raising the teacup to her lips.

The back door slammed open, and a wave of cold air rushed in, chilling the room. Travis stood in the doorway. "Sarah's in labor."

~

Wyatt sat in front of the fire. He'd gotten home earlier in the day, and just as he'd thought, his men had all the animals secure. They were happy to see him, but he didn't have to worry. They had everything under control.

He wasn't in the mood for company, and he now sat watching flames consume wood, a drink in his hand.

All he could think about was Eugenia, and that made him angry. They were finished. He'd done exactly as she'd asked, and they hadn't discussed the future until this morning after her boys arrived. And that conversation was short and sweet. She wasn't going to marry him, but he was good enough for a quick tumble once a week.

And God help him, he loved the woman. The past two days had cemented what his heart already knew. He loved that stubborn gray-haired woman with the flashing blue eyes. Loved her and wanted to marry her.

He slammed the empty glass on the table beside him and poured another shot of whiskey into the tumbler.

Gus walked in. "What are you doing?"

"Drinking."

"I see that. It's only three o'clock in the afternoon, and you're already getting drunk," he said, frowning at him, a worried expression on his weathered face.

Wyatt didn't respond. What was the point? He only wanted to get drunk.

"Exactly where were you these last few days?" Gus asked.

For a moment Wyatt didn't say a word, knowing he couldn't tell Gus everything. The man gossiped worse than any woman he'd ever met. "I was in a line shack not far from the Burnett place."

"Alone?"

Wyatt paused. "Yeah, just me and some mice sharing a cabin."

The memory of Eugenia curled naked around him came to mind, and he couldn't say a word. Nothing. Naught. Perhaps it was better this way. This way no one would know that she'd turned him down. This way he could lick his wounds in private. This way he could heal his battered heart.

"I bet that was cold and lonely."

"Yes," he said, hating lying but knowing it was best.

"You still pining over Mrs. Burnett?" Gus asked, his voice suspicious.

Wyatt gazed at the weathered face of his friend and wished the man would go away and leave him in peace. Today was his day to mourn the end of his hopes and dreams with Eugenia. Today was his to nurse his broken heart.

Tomorrow he would once again be his chipper self, but not today. Not now. Not when his wounds felt exposed, his chest open, his heart ruptured and bleeding.

"I'm not pining over Eugenia."

"Then what's got you in this funk? The only other time I saw you with a whiskey glass in your hand at three o'clock in the afternoon was when Mrs. Beatrice died. Who died?" Gus asked raising his brows.

For a moment, Wyatt just stared at Gus. "Don't you have something to do?"

Gus pondered, completely ignoring Wyatt's comment. "How's that church play thingie going? You and Eugenia still getting along?"

"You are not going to be satisfied until you pry out whatever you think is bothering me, are you? Should I make up something?" Wyatt asked as he took another sip of his whiskey.

Gus grinned. "Wouldn't be a good friend if I didn't try to figure what's got you so determined to become booze blind." Eugenia's got you in a horn-tossin' mood."

"Forget the name Eugenia," he warned Gus.

"No casseroles in the last few days, although the weather put everything on hold," Gus stated, and Wyatt wanted to rip the words from Gus's throat. The man was a determined irritant.

"The casseroles are done. There won't be any more casseroles," he said, wondering what Eugenia was doing today.

"What about Eugenia? You still think she's the one?"

"She's the one about as much as you are. Now get on out of here before I do something really stupid like fire you," he said, his voice raised loud enough that even his sleeping dogs lifted their heads and glanced at him in annoyance.

"Yes, sir. We've been together more than twenty years, and you're letting a woman come between us," Gus said, putting his hands up in the air and stepping back.

Wyatt closed his eyes and let his head roll from side to side. "I apologize, Gus. But I just want to sit here and drink myself into oblivion this afternoon."

"Apology accepted. That doesn't mean I'm not going to worry about you. I'll check back in on you later to see if you're still sitting up right," Gus said, backing out of the room.

"How many times have you seen me that drunk?" Wyatt said, raising his voice.

"Never. That's why I'm concerned."

"You don't have to worry. I'm just drinking long enough for the pain to be dulled. Once the pain is dulled then I'll go to bed."

"She's not worth the way you're going to feel in the morning," Gus said.

"Maybe not. But I'm just getting through today," Wyatt said and took another drink."

Chapter Ten

The ride from the house into town was quiet. The roads were still snowy and treacherous, but at least Eugenia could see where other people had traveled.

One of Tucker's deputies had ridden out to find him to let him know that Sarah was in labor. He'd left immediately, and now the rest of the family was following.

Her heart pounded in her chest, filled with elation to see the new baby. Eugenia was torn between her excitement and despair. She missed Wyatt. She missed his nearness and knew if she'd agreed to marry him, he would have been by her side for this important family event. And now, her children thought her a fool for not accepting Wyatt's offer.

When they arrived at the house, Eugenia found Tucker inside pacing the floor, anxiously looking for them. "Mom, we can't find old Doc Wilson. He's not made it back into town."

"Let me talk to Sarah, son," Eugenia said, calmly trying to ease Tucker's fears.

Eugenia walked into the bedroom and saw Sarah in the middle of a contraction, standing, hanging onto the bedpost, breathing harshly, her face contorted with pain.

Rose came in behind Eugenia and walked over to Sarah and rubbed her back. "You doing okay?"

At the end of the contraction, Sarah took several deep breaths. "I'm so glad all of you are here. I don't think the doctor is going to make it. My contractions are getting stronger, so I know the time is almost here. Tucker said he could do it, but I just want to make sure he has help."

She turned and gazed at Eugenia. "I think it would be special if you delivered your grandchild."

Eugenia couldn't help but smile. "Thank you, Sarah. But if Tucker's up to it, I think he should deliver his child."

Sarah smiled and grabbed onto the bed post. "I feel another one coming. It hasn't been that long…"

When the contraction had finished, she lay down in the bed. "I had Kira prepare everything that we need. It's all laid out on the table."

Tucker walked into the bedroom. "How are you doing?"

"We're getting close. Your mother said that you should deliver the baby. Are you okay with that?"

He leaned down and kissed his wife on the top of her head. "I'll do whatever you need me to do. You're the doctor."

"Yeah, but I can't deliver my own child."

"We can do this," Eugenia said, patting her daughter-in-law's hand. She'd delivered a baby years ago and was excited to help Sarah.

Just then another contraction began, and Sarah grabbed her husband's hand. "Oh God, this one is going to be a bad one. I've…I've got to push. It may be time."

Eugenia raised Sarah's nightgown. "Nothing yet. Come on, push, Sarah."

"Aargh…" Sarah screamed. "Aargh! It's coming. I can feel him."

Eugenia glanced again. "Oh my gosh, I can see its little head. You're doing great. Son, if you're going to deliver this baby, you need to get down here."

Rose stood on one side of the bed, and she wiped down Sarah's face with a cool cloth. "It's almost over. Hang in there, Sarah."

Tucker released his wife's hand and went down to the end of the bed. He took one look at his child's head crowning, and he passed out cold.

Eugenia caught him and gently laid him down on the floor.

"This is why men don't belong in the birthing room," she said under her breath.

"Is he all right?" Sarah cried in between short breaths.

"He's fine," Eugenia said, her focus on her daughter-in-law and her new grandchild. Her son would be fine once he awoke. "Come on, Sarah, one more push and this baby will be here. Push hard."

Sarah screamed as she pushed, and the baby slid into the hands of its grandmother.

"Oh my gosh, it's a girl! A baby girl," Eugenia cried, holding the infant in her arms. "A sweet, precious, baby girl."

Rose handed her a damp cloth, and she wiped off the infant's face. The baby began to howl in protest, screaming, her eyes glued tightly shut, her arms and legs flailing.

Eugenia began to cry, her eyes flooding with tears as she gazed on her fourth grandchild. "Another granddaughter. She's beautiful."

A moan came from the floor, and Tucker raised up. "What happened?"

Realizing what was going on, he jumped to his feet. "Did I miss it?"

Eugenia wrapped up the crying baby and handed her to Tucker. "Show your wife your new child while I deliver the afterbirth and clean Sarah up.

A few minutes later, Rose and Eugenia walked out of the room, leaving the couple to enjoy a few minutes alone with their new daughter.

When Eugenia stepped out into the living room, Travis and Tanner looked at them expectantly, and she burst into tears. The last few days caught up with her, and she sat down in a chair and cried.

Rose smiled and told the waiting men. "Baby and mother are fine. Eugenia brought her new granddaughter into the world. We're giving the new parents a few minutes alone to get acquainted with their daughter."

~

Several hours later, Eugenia sat in the bedroom watching the baby suckle at Sarah's breast.

"Dammit, Mother!" Tucker exclaimed quietly. "You won't even let us pay you respect by naming the baby after you and Sarah's mother."

"I'm not sticking my beautiful granddaughter with my name. You may choose my middle name, but please do not give her the name Eugenia. I appreciate what you're doing, but I love this child too much to saddle her with this monstrosity. She would hate me."

Sarah laughed from the bed, gazing with love at her baby daughter. "Thank you, Eugenia. I love you, but your name is a mouthful. It sounds more like a country than a woman's name."

"See, my daughter-in-law appreciates me. Ellen Marie would be a lovely name for my granddaughter."

Tucker gazed at his wife, and she smiled at him and nodded her head. "I think it's lovely."

He ran his hand over his daughter's fuzzy head. "Welcome to the world, Ellen Marie. Please don't inherit your grandmother's stubbornness, or we could have problems. I'm your daddy, and I'm the marshal, so listen up."

The baby snuggled in closer to Sarah, her mouth all pouty after her feeding.

"Thank you for naming her after me. It means so much to me that I delivered my granddaughter and was the first one to see her sweet, precious face," Eugenia said, her emotions bubbling to the surface like a hot apple pie.

A day that had started out wonderful and turned harrowing was once again beautiful. It would forever be memorable. This granddaughter's birthday would be remembered as the day that Wyatt ended their relationship, and that left Eugenia sad until the baby arrived.

It was a mixed blessings kind of day.

"Will you stay here a few days and help Sarah until she's feeling better?" Tucker asked.

Eugenia smiled. She needed something to keep her busy and her mind off her loss. Sarah and the baby would be a welcome distraction.

"Of course, I will. The Christmas play is the day after tomorrow on Christmas Eve. I'd be glad to help out," she said, suddenly dreading the play. The idea of seeing Wyatt again made her chest ache. She missed him. Tears pricked her eyes, and she swallowed, holding them back.

Sarah glanced at her husband. "Did you tell your mother we invited Wyatt to Christmas dinner?"

Oh no! How could she see him again without crying?

Eugenia's chest and lungs squeezed tightly at the sound of his name and the possibility he would come to dinner.

Tucker shook his head. "He declined. Said thank you, but he couldn't come."

She wanted to see him. She missed him. She wanted to tell him about baby Ellen. She wanted to tell him about Sarah. She wanted to wrap her arms around him and kiss him until they were both breathless.

Eugenia stood. "It's just as well the old coot doesn't come. He would have eaten all the turkey."

She walked out of the room, her eyes watering, her vision filled with tears that seemed to spring out of nowhere. Why was she so emotional these past few days? Every little thing made her cry.

There was a restlessness in her soul that wouldn't let go. She felt bereft, as if she'd lost her best friend. And she had. She'd lost Wyatt.

~

The night of the Christmas Eve play was bitterly cold with the wind howling out of the north and sending the parishioners hurrying into the warm church.

Wyatt stood in the door wishing everyone a merry Christmas as they entered the building, avoiding the back where the children were lining up for the play. If he went back there, he'd see Eugenia, and he needed to avoid her as much as possible.

After the days of lovemaking, the pain of her rejection was enough to convince him that maybe he should rethink his decision to remarry. Maybe he wasn't meant for marriage. Maybe he should stay alone.

He smiled at the people streaming into the church, and when everyone was seated, he went to check on the wise men. When he entered the curtained off area away from the other kids, he found them slipping on their robes.

"Okay guys, does everyone remember their lines?"

They nodded.

"You guys look ready," he said, thinking only one more hour and this would all be behind him.

"My stomach hurts," Frank said. "I think I'm going to throw up."

The kid's face was chalky white and pale. He couldn't get sick. It had to be a bad case of nerves.

"No, you're going to be fine, Frank. It's nerves. When you get out there, don't look at the people in the audience. Just look at the other players. You'll do great," Wyatt reassured the boy.

Suddenly the kid began to make retching noises, and Wyatt grabbed a bucket and put it under the child and leaned him over.

"It's okay, son. Just relax."

The boy finished throwing up just about the time that Eugenia threw open the curtain. "What's wrong?"

"Frank is feeling a little puny. But you're okay now, right boy?"

The youngster coughed. "Yes, sir. I feel better."

Eugenia looked at Frank and then at Wyatt. In the space of that look, he wanted to grab her and cover her mouth with his. He wanted to remind her of the love they'd experienced, but instead he looked at Frank, keeping his distance.

"You're going to be okay?" Eugenia asked the child.

"It's just a bad case of nerves, and he has it under control now. Right, Frank?"

"I'm okay," the boy said, smiling.

"Good. Everyone needs to take their places," Eugenia said, rushing off.

Wyatt watched her walk away and felt like part of his heart went with her. He patted Frank on the arm. "You sure you're going to make it?"

The boy grinned. "I think so."

"Then let's get the wise men lined up."

The music started, and the narrator began to read the story of Christmas. Wyatt stood right inside the curtain where he could watch the play but also keep an eye on the children. Eugenia was directing, but this way he could see everything without being close to her. He had to keep his distance. He had to protect his heart. He had to give her what she wanted even when he didn't want to.

Mary and Joseph came out riding a live borrowed donkey, and soon they were ensconced in the barn. And then magically a baby appeared in Mary's arms, and the story went on. The angels went on stage next and finally the wise men.

All of the children were on stage except for Wyatt's three wise-ass boys. The play would soon be over, and his involvement with Eugenia would draw to a close. He could rest easy knowing that this would be behind him.

Sure, they'd see each other in town, but keeping his distance would be easier.

"Wyatt?" Eugenia said, coming up next to him.

"Yes?" he whispered, refusing to look at her. He was not going to give her the time of day if possible. He had to protect his heart.

"I want to apologize for the other day."

"No apologies are necessary," he said, still refusing to look at her.

"I don't feel right about what happened between us," she said. "Please, can we talk about this after the program?"

He shook his head, his heart splintering. He wanted nothing more than to say yes, but until she agreed to marry him, there was nothing more to say.

"No. All the talking has been done. I'm going home afterwards."

"Oh," she said, seeming surprised. "So, I guess it's over then."

"Yes, ma'am, I believe it is," he said, still watching the play, not looking at her. Inside, his chest was cracking like ice in spring, fracturing and splintering to pieces. He wanted nothing more than to take her in his arms and tell her that he didn't want it to end. He wanted their life together to be beginning.

A trumpet announced the arrival of the wise men bearing gifts for the new born child, and the donkey brayed wildly. The jackass butted Joseph, sending him into Mary and the baby before running across the stage, his eyes frantic as he searched for an exit. He clomped down the steps and out the back of the church.

For a moment, Wyatt was stunned and so were the children. The audience roared until Frank began to sing

"We Three Kings" and the choir joined him as they sang the song.

"Excuse me, I have to go find an ass," Wyatt said, grateful for any reason to escape Eugenia.

~

After the play, the family gathered at Sarah and Tucker's home. The new baby slept soundly. The other children were running around excited, eagerly awaiting Santa Claus.

Her sons and their wives were sitting on the couch talking and she watched them, happy to see her boys and their families together celebrating the holidays. They were married, and they were happy. She had grandchildren. So why did she feel so sad?

The Christmas play had been a success, even with the unhappy donkey. The children had presented her with a gift at the end. Still, she hadn't felt the same fulfillment this year. Sure, she'd enjoyed working with the children, but after tonight's performance, her chest felt heavy, and she knew why.

Wyatt Jones. He'd barely looked in her direction today. He'd avoided her, and when she'd finally pinned him down, he'd told her they were done.

She'd made her decision, and he was no longer pursuing. And now her heart was breaking at the finality of it all. Her chest ached with a loneliness she'd never experienced. How could she marry Wyatt? How could she let another man take control of her life again? How could she give him the power?

"Mom, are you okay?" Travis asked.

"I'm fine. Just sitting here thinking of Christmases past. And how blessed we are to have a new member of the family."

Yet even tonight, Wyatt had conceded the play to her when everyone asked about the production. Over and over again, she'd heard him tell everyone that he was just a helper, that she'd done it all.

He'd even taken care of Frank when the boy had become ill and made sure that the wise men made it on stage.

It suddenly occurred to her that Wyatt was a caregiver and Thomas had been a caretaker. The difference in the two men was that one was giving, and one was always taking.

Could a man and a woman have a real partnership where they both gave and took? She glanced around at her sons and their wives. Is this what they were doing? Taking care of one another?

"So tell me-in each of your families-who makes the decisions?" she suddenly asked.

They looked at her as if she'd sprouted three heads. Finally Rose, who always seemed to understand her, said, "Travis and I make major decisions together. But I trust him to make decisions about the ranch since he knows cattle and I don't. I guess you could say I trust him to take care of our family."

Travis nodded his head. "Rose is my wife, and I depend on her judgment. She sees things differently than I do, and she's the person I turn to when I have doubts and don't know what to do."

Beth smiled. "It's the same with us. Tanner may be the husband, but we're a team, and we make decisions together that will affect our family."

Tanner reached over and kissed her on the cheek. "My wife is my life, and I couldn't imagine making a major decision without her support and love."

Sarah glanced down at the baby in her arms. "Since the day we married, we made a vow to each other to always work out our problems. Tucker helps me make decisions about my medical practice, and he knows I don't want him to take any unnecessary risks in his job. We're a family, and he may be the head, but I'm the neck, and I support the head."

Eugenia laughed at the way her medical doctor daughter-in-law phrased her response.

Tucker smiled at his wife and kissed the top of their baby's head. "I just do what my wife tells me to do because it makes her happy."

They all laughed, and Eugenia felt a piercing in her chest. Her children had done so much better than she had at this love thing. They were happy, and they had good spouses that she'd helped pick. They were married couples who worked together. What did she have?

"Mom, did you and Dad work together like us?" Tanner asked.

She laughed at the idea of her and Thomas working together. Their life had been good, but they'd never been a team. "No. If he were still alive, our marriage would be different. But I think the reason I can say that is because I'm not the woman he married. I'm so much stronger. I look around at my daughters-in-law, and I'm so grateful you married my sons. You're strong, vibrant women who won't let my boys get away with not working as a family, and I admire that in all of you."

Rose stared at Eugenia. "You could have that, too."

Eugenia stopped and considered her words.

"I think if you gave Wyatt even half a chance, he would give you the world, but not insist on his way all the time. As long as he was by your side, he'd be happy," Rose said quietly.

Eugenia loved this girl who'd never had a family life of her own until Travis.

Rose looked at her. "Or would you rather spend the rest of your life alone? Never experiencing the love you obviously wanted for your children?"

Eugenia stopped. Was that true?

Why wasn't she taking this chance? Did she want to live the rest of her life alone? Why couldn't she let go of the past and give Wyatt a chance? Why was she letting Thomas keep her from finding love again?

They said people died from broken hearts. Now she understood why. Now she knew the true meaning of love. She put her head in her hands.

"Mom?" Travis asked and put his hand on her shoulder.

"I'm the biggest damn fool. I let a good man get away from me."

~

Christmas morning Wyatt sat drinking coffee, reading a book while he waited for the men to gather for Christmas lunch. Since his wife's death, they gathered in the barn to celebrate, and the cook made lunch for everyone.

This morning he sat wondering what Eugenia was doing, his heart filled with sadness that she'd refused to see how their life together would have been good. That was the past, and he'd made the decision to move on, though it would take a while to get back to normal. He doubted he could look at Eugenia again and not feel sadness that she'd thrown away his love.

He took a sip of coffee, hearing his hounds howling. The sun was shining bright, but the temperature was cold outside. This wasn't a simple alert to warn off a varmint. No this was a warning. He stood and glanced out the window and saw two buggies coming down the lane.

Burnett buggies. His heart started beating wildly, but his mind refused to give hope. What the hell was going on?

He strode to the door and threw it open. The preacher was with them? Travis Burnett pulled the brake on the wagon and then helped his mother down. She reached back into the wagon and pulled something out.

A casserole dish.

For a moment, his heart stopped, and then she came to the door where he stood waiting while her family remained in the buggy.

She stopped before him. "Merry Christmas, Wyatt."

"Merry Christmas, Eugenia," he said, looking down at the dish, wondering if his old heart could take the disappointment if this didn't mean what he hoped it meant.

She stared at him, her blue eyes misty with tears.

"What's that?"

"The last casserole any woman's bringing you."

His heart was pounding so hard he almost felt faint. "That's a great Christmas present, Eugenia. The best."

She held up her hand. "Let me say my piece." She took a deep breath. "Sometimes I'm a stubborn woman who doesn't know what she wants until she's lost it. I had to learn to let go of the past and remember that I'm a different woman today than I was twenty-five years ago. I'm stronger. I'm better."

He nodded but didn't say anything. She had to tell him. She had to say the words or there could be nothing.

"If you promise me that our marriage would be a partnership with both of us making the decisions-neither one answering for the other-then I want to spend the rest of my life with you."

"Oh, Eugenia," he said, gathering her up in his arms and hugging her to his chest. "God, I never thought you would come to your damn senses."

Against his chest she said, "I love you, Wyatt Jones, and these last few days without you have been hard. I've missed you more than my next breath. Please tell me you still want to marry me."

He pushed her arms out and looked into her eyes. "Right now. Right this minute," he said, kissing her on the lips.

Cheers and applause could be heard coming from the wagons, and Wyatt felt like his soul was rejoicing. He broke the kiss.

"Oh, hell, honey, I've been waiting for your casserole for months. Took you long enough."

"I know, Wyatt. I brought the preacher man along if you're serious about getting married," she said, a wistful hesitancy in her voice.

He laughed. "Tell them to come on in and let's get this wedding started."

"Can we go back to Tucker and Sarah's for Christmas lunch? I'd like to spend our first holiday together with my family."

"If that's what you want, that's what we'll do," he said, excited enough that he could barely keep from jumping up and down. He thought he'd burst from happiness.

She smiled up at him and caressed the side of his face with her hand. "I woke up this morning and wanted with all my heart to be your Christmas bride."

"I love you, Eugenia. I would have made you a bride months ago, sweetheart."

The End

Thank You For Reading!

Dear Reader,

I hope you enjoyed *The Christmas Bride* as much as I enjoyed writing it!

I have one small request. If you're inclined, please leave a review. Whether or not you loved the book or hated it-I'd enjoy your feedback. Reviews are difficult to obtain and have the power to make or break a book.

Reading one of my books is like spending time with me, and I just want to say Thank you from the bottom of my heart.

Sincerely,
Sylvia McDaniel

Books by Sylvia McDaniel

Contemporary Romance

Standalones
The Reluctant Santa
My Sister's Boyfriend
The Wanted Bride
The Relationship Coach
Her Christmas Lie
Secrets, Lies, and Online Dating
Paying for the Past
Cupid's Revenge

Anthologies
Kisses, Laughter & Love
Christmas with you

Collaborative Series

Magic, New Mexico
Touch of Decadence

Western Historicals

Standalones
A Hero's Heart
A Scarlet Bride
Second Chance Cowboy

The Cuvier Women
Wronged
Betrayed
Beguiled

Lipstick and Lead
Desperate
Deadly
Dangerous
Daring
Determined
Deceived

Scandalous Suffragettes
Abigail
Bella
Callie
Faith

The Burnett Brides
The Rancher Takes a Bride
The Outlaw Takes a Bride
The Marshal Takes a Bride
The Christmas Bride

Anthologies
Wild Western Women
Courting the West
Wild Western Women Ride Again

Collaborative Series

The Surprise Brides
Ethan

American Mail Order Brides
Katie

About the Author

Sylvia McDaniel is a best-selling, award-winning author of historical romance and contemporary romance novels. Known for her sweet, funny, family-oriented romances, Sylvia is the author of The Burnett Brides, a western historical western series, The Cuvier Widows, a Louisiana historical series, and several short contemporary romances.

She is the former President of the Dallas Area Romance Authors, a member of the Romance Writers of America®, and a member of Novelists Inc. Her novel, A Hero's Heart, was a 1996 Golden Heart Finalist. Several other books have placed or won in the San Antonio Romance Authors Contest and the LERA Contest, and she was a Golden Network Finalist.

Married for nearly twenty years to her best friend, they have two dachshunds that are beyond spoiled and a good-looking, grown son who thinks there's no place like home. She loves gardening, shopping, knitting, and football (Cowboys and Bronco's fan), but not necessarily in that order.

Look for her the first Tuesday of every month at the Plotting Princesses blogspot, and be sure to sign up for her newsletter to learn about new releases and contests. Every month a new subscriber is entered into a drawing for a free book!

She can be found online at: www.sylviamcdaniel.com or on Facebook. You can write to Sylvia at P.O. Box 2542, Coppell, TX 75019.

Looking for a new book to read?

Check out Secrets, Lies, and Online Dating!

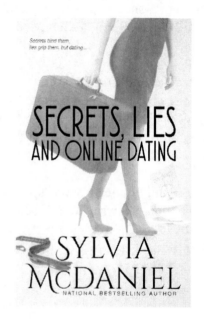

One lie changes the course of three lives...

When Marianne Larson uncovers a truth about her marriage, she sets out to change the course of her life, finding herself along the way. But that journey doesn't come easy as her mother and daughter decide to take a ride of their own–a ride that just might change all of their lives.

While discovering secrets, lies, and the truth about men & dating, three generations and three very different personalities recreate their lives and strengthen their female bond. But what they find might just be what they knew all along...

Sneak Peek into Secrets, Lies, and Online Dating

Marianne Larson stood before the apartment door of her husband's latest fling with his two suitcases in hand, determined, scared, and mad as hell. Birds twittered happy songs in the early spring afternoon in North Dallas, but it could have been a death dirge for all she cared.

Like an overcooked steak, she felt fried, burnt to a crisp –she was emotionally done. She had finally let go of the idea that marriage is forever. Each breath she took felt like a fifty-pound bowling ball resting on her chest.

Marianne dropped the two bulging suitcases onto the concrete walk and waited for the constable to step out of sight. She shoved her blonde hair away from her face, yanked back her shoulders, and lifted her shaking fingers to the doorbell.

Her new life was about to begin.

A shadow filled the peephole, and hushed, panicked voices echoed from inside the apartment. She recognized her adulterous, soon-to-be ex-husband's voice. The door opened as far as the security chain allowed.

A blonde woman peeked through the gap with a too-wide, fake smile. Marianne blinked in disbelief at the girl's thigh high boots, clinging thong, and bustier. A leather whip was still in her hand, the perfect accessory to her dominatrix outfit.

"Marianne! What a surprise."

For a moment, Marianne stared, stunned, before hysterical laughter bubbled up from deep within her. She recognized the girl from the company picnic, but leather? Whips?

At her laughter, the girl's russet eyes darkened.

"Yes, a surprise for both of us. I never knew Daniel was into…" Marianne stumbled over the word "…games."

She gathered her wits. "I brought Daniel his clothes."

The woman's dark eyes widened. "Here? Whatever for?"

"Look, I know Daniel is inside. His BMW is in the parking lot. You're not the first one to climb on top of him while earning a promotion, though I see you have a unique way of securing your advancement."

Daniel's reddened face appeared in the doorway, his body hidden by his dominatrix. "Marianne, what are you doing here?"

"Bringing you your clothes."

Marianne gazed upon her college sweetheart, her heart void of the love it once held. Daniel shoved his lover aside, slid back the security chain, and yanked the door open.

"Honey, you know this means nothing."

The view of her husband with a leather choke collar around his neck and a leather thong clinging to his loins brought uncontrollable laughter spewing from her like a fountain. How could she not have known that he was into sexual games?

The constable standing to the side muffled his snicker.

"You're right. Your cheating means nothing anymore."

Daniel flinched.

She handed the bulging suitcases to the man she'd once loved.

"Here are your things," Marianne said, trembling from nerves, though she'd never felt more certain in her life. "And Constable Warren has something for you."

The constable stepped into the breezeway. "Are you Daniel Larson?"

"Yes?"

The officer shoved the paperwork into Daniel's hand. "Consider yourself served."

"Marianne?" Daniel questioned, his voice rising as he tore open the envelope. "What the hell is this?"

"It's called a divorce. You've cheated on me for the last time."

His dark eyes widened as he scanned the contents of the document.

Daniel lifted his shocked gaze to her. "You can't be serious! You locked me out of our home?"

"Yes. I'll see you in court," she said, wanting to escape before the scene turned ugly.

His tone became cajoling. "Marianne, honey, we've been married a long time. Because of me, you live a comfortable life. You *need* me to take care of you."

God, no wonder Daniel was top salesman year after year. "You know, that line worked the first hundred times you used it, but not any longer. I'm done, Daniel."

Marianne walked off, certain they'd said everything.

Daniel followed her, barefoot, his dog chain clinking on the ground. At noon, most people were at work, but a few stopped to stare.

"Don't do this, Marianne. Think of our daughter."

She kept marching, each determined step finishing what she should have ended years ago.

"I'll end the affair. I'll change," Daniel promised.

Marianne whirled around to face him. "Why?"

He stopped, his chain rattling, his expression perplexed by her question. "Because – because you want me to."

"Do I?" She paused, considering his remark for a few seconds. "And that would last until the next pretty blonde in your office offered you a little booty, and then you'd cheat again."

Daniel stood half-naked in the open parking lot, a baffled expression on his handsome face. He didn't seem to know how to react.

"Don't do this," Daniel begged. "I won't give you a divorce."

"Fine. I wanted to make this quick and to protect our

daughter from knowing the truth about her father, but we can do this the hard way. A long, drawn-out legal trial will force me to parade your extra-marital affairs through the courtroom. In the end, I'll be entitled to sixty percent of our assets instead of the normal fifty. And our daughter will know what a douche bag her father is."

His dark eyes burned her. "You wouldn't dare."

"And this little escapade will make for interesting viewing in the courtroom. Wave at the camera, darling."

The detective she'd hired moved from behind the van and waved at him, the red light of the video camera beamed as it recorded his stunned expression. Part of her felt despicable for being so brutal, but the rational part knew he deserved this and more. This time he would not brainwash her into believing she had no choice but to stay.

"You planned this," he said in awe.

"Yes, I did," she admitted, proud that she had pushed aside her fears and done what should have happened years ago.

Daniel gave her a pleading look that reached inside, igniting all the fear locked away. Never again would she return to being the same wife who had tolerated his cheating for at least three years.

"Marianne," his voice changed to the sweet seductive tone that normally convinced her to see things his way. "We've been married a long time, baby. You don't play these kinds of games with me. We have a good life together. We have a daughter."

"I want out."

"You've spent the last eighteen years a stay-at-home mom. Are you going to get a job?" He tried to take her hand, but she stepped out of his reach. "Who's going to hire an older woman with no skills?"

CPSIA information can be obtained
at www.ICGtesting.com
Printed in the USA
LVOW10s2238011117
554590LV00001B/29/P